C000212786

THE DRAGON'S NEED

Tahoe Dragon Mates #2

JESSIE DONOVAN

Mythical Lake Press, LLC

This book is a work of fiction. Names, characters, places, and incidents are either the product of the writer's imagination or are used fictitiously, and any resemblance to actual persons, living or dead, business establishments, events, or locales is entirely coincidental.

Want to stay up to date on releases? Please join my newsletter by clicking here to sign-up.

Books in this series:

Tahoe Dragon Mates
The Dragon's Choice (TDM #1)
The Dragon's Need (TDM #2)
The Dragon's Bidder / Wes & Ashley (TDM #3 / July 16, 2020)

The Dragon's Need Synopsis

Tired of overprotective dragon-shifters, Gabriela Santos decides she wants to lose her virginity to a human male via the Tahoe area dragon lottery. After years of trying, she's finally selected as one of the participants. Of the hundreds of humans who want to be with her, it's the male staring at the ceiling who catches her eye. And after a bit of honesty and insight into why he's there, she picks him. However, soon one kiss changes her future forever.

Only to try and forget his cheating ex-wife does Ryan Ford agree to enter the dragon lottery. He has no expectations of the dragonwoman walking the aisles to pick him. However, when his mind wanders and he becomes lost in thought, the dragon lady calls him out on it. Her straightforward manner and wit is refreshing. Add in the instant spark between them, and Ryan agrees to sleep with her to try to give her a baby. But then one kiss brings out her inner dragon, and Ryan quickly learns that he's her true mate and has to accept a frenzy or try running away.

As the pair come to terms with their fate, they soon start falling for one another. But when someone targets Ryan, will he survive and find a way for them to be together? Or will he have to leave both Gabriela and his unborn child to stay alive?

NOTE: This is a quick, steamy standalone story about fated mates and sexy dragon-shifters near Lake Tahoe in the USA. You don't have to read all my other dragon books to enjoy this one!

Chapter One

G abriela Santos stepped into a hotel ballroom in South Lake Tahoe and did her best to remain calm.

Even though she'd secretly been entering the dragon lottery for years—her brother thought it had only been once—hoping to be chosen, her nerves still threatened to show now that she was about to start her life-changing journey.

As she gave a cursory glance at the couple of hundred men—*human* men—all sitting in rows, looking at her with curiosity and occasionally lust, she nearly gave a nervous laugh.

After so many years of dragon-shifter males saying she was too headstrong, too idealistic, too human, it was strange that so many men were gathered for the chance of sleeping with her.

Her inner dragon, the other half of her personality,

spoke up and huffed. *Of course they should be here. It's not our fault the dragon males were too overprotective, too domineering to notice or want us. These humans do.*

Which Gaby knew, of course. And yet… *They may be here by choice, but one of them is going to be in for something more than they'd bargained for.*

Gaby was probably the only twenty-four-old dragon-shifter virgin among the four dragon clans near Lake Tahoe.

Her beast grunted. *That is all your fault, not mine. How I've stayed sane this long despite you denying what we need, I'll never understand.*

Guilt tugged at her heart. Inner dragons needed sex on a regular basis. To them, it was as necessary as eating and breathing.

Still, she took a deep breath and managed to get out, *I couldn't give in to one of them. At first, they just wanted to lose their virginity. And as we got older, they saw us only as a conquest. Thanks, but no thanks.*

And how is that different than these men?

At least these men won't expect anything afterward, such as free reign to growl and tell others how to treat me.

Not all dragon-shifter males were unbearable, but any of the decent ones who saw a mating as a partnership instead of the male thinking he had every right to protect her without her input were rare.

Really rare, at least in her experience. Maybe if her clan interacted more with the other three dragon clans in the area, she might've found someone.

No, the human males in the room were her best chance at losing her virginity, having a child, and sculpting her own future on her terms.

Her beast replied, *For all you know, you could pick one who acts the same way.*

Ah, but it's only sex and then it's done. That's a situation I can control. It's not forever.

Unless you find your true mate.

Gaby mentally snorted. *Right, because that happens so often at these things. Given how Jose found his true mate a month ago, it's more likely I'd win a jackpot in Reno than find him here.*

While she was happy for her older brother, she couldn't help being a little jealous. A true mate was a dragon-shifter's best chance for happiness. Not a guarantee, but better odds than with a random stranger.

Her dragon replied, *He could be here. And before you protest some more, remember that the strongest human males will mate a dragonwoman. It's not impossible.*

Strongest not just physically, but mentally as well. *Well, there aren't any human male mates in the four clans in the Tahoe area, so let's just treat this for what it is, okay? We'll have a child of our own and can live our lives without a male trying to guard us every second of every day.*

Maybe. But what happens if we die on a firefighting assignment?

Gaby had worked for years to become one of the local firefighters, belonging to the only contingent that included both humans and dragon-shifters. She replied,

A child will give us something even stronger to fight for to stay alive, right? Besides, our family will help. You know they will.

Her inner beast sighed. *Of course.*

Whenever her dragon was so easily complacent, Gaby knew she didn't really agree and wanted to say more.

However, before she could pry, the American Department of Dragon Affairs—or ADDA—employee named Ashley Swift reached the podium and waited for the room to quiet.

Ignoring her pounding heart, Gaby focused on Ashley instead of the hundreds of men in the room. She could do with a minute or two to gather her courage and be who she usually was—a confident young dragonwoman who had learned long ago not to take anyone's shit.

Ashley finally spoke, her voice echoing in the room from various speakers. "Welcome to the Lake Tahoe Dragon Lottery. Each of you applied and passed the screening process, so congratulations. You've made it here, which is a good sign. However, I will give you all one last chance to leave without facing any sort of consequence from backing out. Think on this wisely because once this next minute is up, you're committed to the contracts you signed. And the minute to make a dash out the door begins…now."

Gaby forced herself to watch the room. A few men stood and walked out without saying a word.

For a split second, she wondered if it was because they took one look at her and said no way.

But then she pushed it aside. If they were that shallow, then it was their problem, not hers.

When the minute ended, Ashley spoke again. "Okay, those guys are clearly not meant to be here and ADDA will have to work harder at screening in the future. Regardless, we'll continue. In case you forgot, you're to stay seated while Gabriela walks around the room, asking questions and determining who she'll pick. You're not to talk unless she asks you something. If you break any of the rules, you'll be escorted out." Ashley narrowed her eyes and looked around the room. "I've done this before and if you think you're above the rules and decide catcalling is going to somehow lure Gaby to you, then you'll be taken out of here quicker than you can snap your fingers." Ashley stood tall again and looked at Gaby. "The room is yours."

Gaby hadn't spent too much time with Ashley Swift until recently, but the more she learned about the human, the more Gaby liked her.

Nodding, Gaby turned toward the room and somehow made her feet work, heading toward the front row.

There were so many men, all different ethnicities, ages, and even confidence levels. Some were staring at the ground, others at her, and even some at the clock.

Okay, those staring at the clock were moved down the list of those to check out more closely.

Her dragon laughed. *Hey, give them a break. If you were waiting to see if your future would change forever, you might look at the clock, too, to remember when it happened.*

Right, because that's why they're doing it.

You never know. After all, they are *human. A lot of times their actions don't make sense to me.*

Gaby bit her lip to keep from smiling at her dragon's pitying tone. *Shush, or I'll never be able to do this.*

I'll be here, if you need me.

As her dragon curled up and laid her head on her forelimbs at the back of her mind, Gaby took comfort from the everyday action. She loved her inner dragon, but there was only one thing she couldn't do that a male's dragon could do—instantly realize if their true mate was in the room.

Yet another way females were at a disadvantage with dragon-shifters, in addition to being smaller in size in their dragon forms and not quite as strong.

Focus, Gaby. Right, she could do this. And so she turned all her attention to the men.

Maybe she should ask more questions as she walked by, but she wanted to move around first so she could at least glimpse everyone and then start winnowing them down to make her decision.

A few of the faces looked familiar. Of course there was a chance she'd seen them in South Lake Tahoe before. Her work's headquarters was based here, after all. Even if she mostly worked the surrounding forests, she still came to the city on occasion.

And yet, as a bearded face, another with stubble, one clean-shaven, and so on passed by, she had no idea how to choose. A handsome guy could turn into an asshole when he opened his mouth. And one of the quiet ones could turn out to be the male she'd always dreamed of.

Maybe she'd suggest in the future about how ADDA could give the dragon-shifter candidates portfolios of all the males beforehand, to help sort through them.

As Gaby reached the back of the large room, she noticed a dark-haired male with his hands behind his head, supporting it as he looked at the ceiling.

She couldn't decide if that was worse than looking at the clock.

But she swore she heard a sigh, and it made her curious. So Gaby went to him and drawled, "Bored?"

He jumped a little and met her gaze, his hazel eyes an interesting mix of brown and green.

To his credit, the human male merely shrugged. "It's not every day a guy is treated like a piece of meat, trying to be the best cut on offer."

His accent held the tiniest amount of twang, almost liked he'd grown up in Texas but had left long ago.

Gaby didn't realize she had a weakness for the hint of a twang until just that moment, and she wanted to hear more. "Welcome to what females deal with on a daily basis."

He tilted his head. "Those who treat you that way don't deserve you. It's pretty simple."

Gaby blinked. No excuses, or even apologies. Nope, this human merely said she was worth more.

Both human and dragon took a greater interest.

Not that she was quite ready to make a decision. She needed at least a little more from him first. Glancing down at his name tag she read, "Ryan Ford." She met his gaze. "Well, Ryan, why are you here, then?"

If he was surprised by her question, the human didn't show it. And Gaby barely noticed that she held her breath, waiting to hear his answer.

RYAN FORD still couldn't believe he'd gone through with this damn thing.

His younger sister had hounded him until he'd said yes and promised to go through it all seriously, Tiffany confident that merely attending the lottery would get him thinking about moving on.

As if it were simple to forget your twin brother had stolen your wife and married her a little over a year ago.

No. He sighed. His ex-wife had stolen so many of his years, his heart, his energy, and so much more he didn't want to think about right now. Just wallowing a little was breaking his promise to Tiffany, and he loved his sister too much to do that.

Ryan had been just about to stop staring at the ceiling when the sexy dragon lady had spoken to him.

Maybe Ryan should've been charming, or some other

bullshit. But for some reason, he'd spoken the truth with her. It'd been a long time since he'd felt that at ease with another so quickly.

But then she asked her question, a difficult one, about why he was here.

Again, he should've smiled and been charming, and said he was there to find someone as lovely as her. But his brain and tongue betrayed him and he replied, "Because my little sister thought this would be the best way to move on from the woman who stomped on my heart and smashed it to pieces."

Well, that should make her walk away, shouldn't it? Then he could go back to Phoenix and find some other way to move on with his life.

Although the dragon lady named Gabriela didn't walk away but merely stared at him with her pretty brown eyes, searching his gaze as if determining whether he was telling the truth or not.

Given what he'd heard of dragon-shifters over the years—about being quick-tempered and often more animal than human—it surprised him.

Maybe dragons and humans were more alike than he'd realized.

Then her pupils flashed to slits and back, and he sat up straighter. He'd heard dragon-shifters did that with their eyes when talking with the inner dragon inside them, but he'd never seen it before.

Maybe some would think it weird or alien, but it intrigued him, reminding him how humans and dragons were different in at least one area—the woman in front of him could shift into a giant flying beast.

Gabriela asked, "How long ago did the female break your heart?"

He was aware of the men sitting all around him, no doubt reveling in his secrets or pitying him since most guys would rather chop off an arm than share personal information. But frankly, Ryan didn't give a shit. He'd never understood the need to be secretive and stony. Life was too short to be an asshole for most of it. He'd leave that title to his brother. "Almost two years ago."

"And how old are you?"

The corner of his mouth ticked up. "Tell me your age first, darling."

"Twenty-four."

No hesitation, no admonishing him about asking a woman her age, just the truth.

Ryan leaned forward a little, wanting to talk more with her. "I'm thirty-six."

She might consider him ancient. But as he studied her eyes, which appeared to notice every little thing about him and assessed his every movement, she seemed older than her years.

It was then he noticed more than her eyes. She had dark hair with blonde highlights and light brown skin, skin that he felt the urge to lean over and lick with his tongue.

What? No, stop, Ford. But he couldn't keep from then staring at her mouth, the source of so many intriguing questions and answers. The bottom lip was fuller than the top, and he wanted to stand up, pull her close, and take it between his teeth.

Woah, hold on there. Not only had he just met her, she could pick any of the men in the room. And a slightly bitter divorcee with trust issues would be at the bottom of that list.

Gaby finally nodded, as if making a decision. He met her eyes again, brows drawn. Was she saying yes to him?

However, before he could say a word, she stated, "I want him, Ashley. I want Ryan Ford."

He stopped breathing for a few seconds. All of this had been a way to placate his sister, to get her off his back, and yet the dragon lady had picked him?

Not only that, but the end result of this whole thing would probably make him a father.

Maybe the last part would make the others bolt, but Ryan had wanted to be a dad for a long, long time. He'd held off because of his ex, which had ended up being fortunate.

But having a child that was half this sexy, smart, bold woman?

The image of her round with his child stoked something inside him, a need he hadn't felt before, not even with his ex.

A feeling rushed through him, his gut saying that if he turned her down, he'd regret it for the rest of his life.

He hadn't planned on leaving with a dragonwoman, but now he couldn't imagine leaving without her.

So Ryan stood up and offered his arm, like in the times of old. Amusement danced in Gabriela's eyes, but she threaded her arm through his, making her forearm brush against his.

At the casual contact, heat raced up his arm and down his body, straight to his dick.

He glanced down at her, her pupils flashing quickly, and he wondered if she'd felt it too.

The ADDA employee cleared her throat and said, "Come with me, you two. You can stare deep into one another's eyes later."

Her words snapped him from the spell, and Ryan forced himself to look forward and follow the ADDA employee out of the room.

Now all he had to do was not fuck things up once he was alone with the dragon lady. Because he yearned to learn more about her, and even her dragon half, with each step he took.

Maybe this was the change his life had needed—one he'd never anticipated but now looked forward to.

Chapter Two

G aby's heart pounded as she walked down the hall, her arm through Ryan's.

Their skin had barely brushed yet her entire body was on fire, her clothes suddenly feeling a size too small. The urge to strip him and surrender her virginity without a thought rushed through her body.

Could he be her true mate? After all, Gaby had never had such a strong reaction to a male in her entire life. She may be a virgin, but she'd kissed and fooled around.

None of those times compared to being next to Ryan, breathing in the earthy combination of woods and male, his heat seeping through her clothes.

Her dragon spoke up. *Wishing won't make it so.*

So you don't want him?

Oh, I do. I'd take just about any male with a working cock at this point.

She mentally growled at her inner beast. *You're not*

helping.

Her dragon flicked her wings in the equivalent of a shrug. *You'll find out when he kisses you.*

On the slim chance he was her true mate, she'd have to put off kissing the human until they arrived at the house provided by ADDA for them to, er, get busy. Because when a true mate kicked off a mate-claim frenzy with a kiss, her dragon wouldn't stop demanding sex until they were pregnant.

Which could scare a human all too easily, especially one who had no idea what they were in for.

And yet as she glanced from the corner of her eyes, taking in Ryan's dark stubble, strong jaw, and lips, she wanted him to kiss every inch of her body.

She resisted blinking. At this rate, Gaby wondered if she could keep her lips away from his until they arrived at the ADDA house. Because she wasn't entirely sure she could.

It was as if she were some horny teenager, ready to dive into their first make-out session.

If she were watching this play out to someone else, it'd be almost funny—the virgin finally wanting to jump someone and having to wait or risk giving some ADDA employee a free show.

And while Gaby didn't want flowers and champagne, it wasn't too much for a girl to ask for some privacy for her first time having sex.

Ashley opened a door and motioned them inside a room.

Once inside, Gaby expected Ryan to release her, but he kept her arm firmly in his.

Oh no. Was he yet another alpha male, ready to dictate what she could and couldn't do, just like the dragonmen back on her clan?

Had she made the wrong choice?

Once Ashley joined them in the room, she pointed to two chairs, facing each other across a table. "Sit, go over the paperwork, and let me know when you're done." She handed a cell phone to Ryan. "My number is in there. Call me if you need anything, and I mean it. Don't be that silent, suffering man, the one trying to be brave when he shouldn't. I call those kinds of men dumbasses."

Gaby bit her lip. Yes, she loved the human female more and more.

Ryan took the phone. "I'll try not to be a dumbass, but I think we all are one at some point in our lives, so I can't promise it 100 percent."

Ashley snorted. "You may stand a chance with the dragon-shifters after all."

Gaby's dragon hummed. *Yes, he just might.*

As her beast blasted thoughts of licking his neck, down his chest, and finally down the goody hair trail below his navel, Gaby's cheeks heated. *Stop it.*

Ashley nodded at her and then left them alone, the door clicking closed echoing inside the room.

Ryan finally released her arm, only to pull out the chair and motion for her to sit.

Wanting to set boundaries—he could merely be

trying to be polite, but Gaby had no idea this early on—
she went to the other side and sat in the other chair.

With a shake of his head, Ryan sat down. "You'd
have my mama frowning, for sure, if she were still alive."

Then Gaby felt a split-second of regret. It hadn't
been a power play, but merely manners.

Pushing the feeling aside, she asked, "I'm sorry for
your loss."

He smiled wistfully. "Oh, my mama passed some time
ago, and my dad not long after. Everyone said he died of
a broken heart."

Humans didn't have true mates, but Gaby knew some
of them were lucky enough to find the equivalent.

Would she find hers, too, in this male? Wanting to
learn more about him, she asked, "And what would she
think of you being here with me right now?"

He put his hands out to his side, palms up. "Honestly? I don't know. I suspect as long as you didn't also
leave me for my brother, she'd welcome you with open
arms."

While she was aware the time was ticking for them to
sign and finish the paperwork, Gaby burned to know
what had turned this male somewhat bitter. "Tell me
what happened. And before you protest, you keep hinting
at it. I don't want your past lingering when we're together
and naked."

Leaning back his chair, Ryan crossed his arms over
his chest. Considering he wasn't a dragon-shifter his
broad chest and toned arms called to her. Would he have

a tan line? Or, did he often go out without his shirt, leaving only his ass and dick pale?

Maybe he went into the sun naked at times like she did.

"Gabriela?"

She resisted shaking her head and met his hazel eyes. "Call me Gaby. Everybody does."

"Well, Gaby, there's not a whole lot to tell. My brother—my *identical twin* brother—cheated on me with my wife, and about a year ago, they married and moved across the country."

Her gut said he didn't want apologies or pity. So Gaby merely blurted what came to mind. "Did he always have a thing for her?"

Ryan's dark brows came together. "I don't think so. He was serving in the army when I met her and married her. Of course, I don't know how long the affair went on. For all I know, it could've started on my wedding day since my brother had leave to attend it."

Even though Gaby had zero claim on the male, she wanted to find the female and challenge her to a boxing match. A match Gaby would easily win. "That's pretty fucked up, isn't it?"

He snorted. "That about sums it up." He studied her a second before adding, "And you know what? You're the first person who hasn't tried to give me some sort of life lesson spiel, about how things will get better and how she's not worth it."

She shrugged one shoulder. "Well, while I'm sorry for

all the pain in your life, I'm pretty happy about you being here with me right now and not with her."

As they stared at one another, the room melted away, her heart rate kicked up, and the temperature rose several degrees.

She was lost in his eyes, an interesting mix of brown and green, and yearned to hear more of the laughs and smiles that he'd no doubt once had, given the lines around his eyes and mouth.

Oh, that mouth. Gaby bit her lip, imagining him doing it instead.

Her dragon growled. *Do the boring human stuff so we can stop imagining that and start doing.*

Ryan was the first to speak again. "You're an interesting woman, Gaby. Your honesty is refreshing, for sure."

She grinned. "You haven't even seen some of the most interesting parts of me yet."

He smiled slowly. "Like to keep a man on his toes, do you? Well, I'm not going to be complaining."

Then she imagined him meeting her family, not running for the hills at how forward they were, and she wondered if he would be more than a baby daddy in the end.

If she believed in fate, then maybe Gaby had saved herself for the male truly worth it.

That's such a human thing to think. Sex is sex. From our orgasms alone, you know it feels good. I don't understand why you avoid it.

*I wasn't avoiding it, dragon. I just hadn't found the right guy.
I think now you have.*

Her skin heated more. *Damn it. At this rate, he's going to notice me blushing. I'm hot enough that my tanned skin won't save me now.*

Her beast merely laughed and went back to curling up inside her mind.

Forcing her gaze from Ryan's, Gaby took one of the binders and passed the other to him. "We need to get this done before the two hours are up."

"Considering how much effort went into this whole thing, I can't imagine them just saying, 'Nope, it's one minute past. Go home and see you next year.'"

She rolled her eyes. "Obviously you haven't had to deal with ADDA as much as I have."

"No, I haven't. Do you hate them then?"

Gaby met his eyes again. Many humans thought ADDA a necessary evil, or didn't think about them at all. A dragon could never forget. "Not usually. But it sucks to have to ask their permission for so many things. They don't usually like humans and dragons mixing, unless it's for some sort of benefit to humankind, like with my job."

"Ah, that's right. You're a forest firefighter. It's one of the few things they told us about ahead of time."

She waited for him to say she would have to quit, that her job was to stay home and raise their baby.

But he merely opened his binder. "Well, let's not upset the ADDA gods and get this done." He met her gaze again. "Because I'd at least like the chance to know you a little, Gaby. And to do that, we need some place private, where people won't be listening in."

Her stomach did a little flip at his slightly deeper voice.

Her dragon rose her head. *Just imagine when he's naked and above us.*

Don't you dare flash images right now.

Then hurry your ass up.

For the first time, Gaby regretted all the porn she'd watched online, making it hard not to imagine her and Ryan doing all those things. But she had never planned to be a virgin this long, and a woman got curious.

Well, at least she had stored up a trove of things she wanted to do with the male sitting across from her. And that motivated her to finish the damn paperwork as quickly as possible.

Looking down, she answered, "Then let's each agree not to talk until we finish all the signatures required."

Ryan pretended to zip his lips and throw away the key. It was super corny, but she still smiled.

Maybe if she were lucky, they'd be some laughter before all the sex. She'd always dreamed of having that kind of male.

However, as Ryan looked at his binder and started reading, she did the same. Yet, she couldn't help but glance up every so often to study the human. But then he'd meet her gaze and smile, and she'd look back at her binder.

Each time she signed a page, her heart raced faster. It was all really happening, and soon.

Unlike male dragon-shifters, females didn't have constant access to the human males unless they turned out to be a true mate. She'd only have three days with him until her next fertile peak the following month.

And if after three months there was no baby, the human was free to walk away. The only exception was if there was a mate-claim frenzy, then ADDA would allow it to play out. However, true mates were rare and most likely not in Gaby's favor.

She clutched the pen tighter in her fingers. She wanted more than three days, or nine in total.

Her dragon yawned. *Then make the most of what we have. Don't waste time once we're alone at the ADDA house.*

And right then and there, Gaby agreed with her inner beast.

Oh, she'd let Ryan know she was a virgin, but not until he was all but inside her. No doubt, he'd be too far gone to care.

And once that was done, she could finally explore a male and live out one of her many fantasies.

True, the whole point of the lottery was to conceive a child for her clan. But that didn't mean she couldn't enjoy the process.

So Gaby went back to reading and did her best to ignore Ryan as she went, only caving for a glance every ten minutes or so until she finished.

Chapter Three

As a man of thirty-six, Ryan used to think he'd learned how to control his body and his dick better than a nineteen-year-old boy.

And yet, the entire time he'd sat inside that small room with Gaby, her scent surrounding him and her heated glances making his body temperature rise, he'd been harder than he'd ever been in his life.

Did dragon-shifters emit some sort of special sex hormones? He didn't remember reading anything about it, but he hadn't been the best student, either.

Which meant he had a lot to learn in a short time.

And only three days at a time to better know the dragon lady he wanted to toss on a bed and fuck like there was no tomorrow.

Even now, as he waited on the front step of the house they were to share for the next three days, keeping an eye out for the car Gaby would be riding inside, he was doing his best to tame his raging cock.

With zero success.

It took everything he had not to try and adjust himself again. After all, an ADDA employee sat in a parked car not ten feet away, waiting for Gaby to arrive before leaving him.

They'd been put in separate cars, he'd discovered, for a reason—they'd once again asked if he wanted to back out. There would be a minor fine, but it was the absolute last chance he could flee if he wanted.

While "Hell no" had echoed through his mind, Ryan had been polite. No use pissing off those who would determine if he could remain in Gaby's life once this was all over.

Oh, he was more than a little pessimistic about falling in love and finally finding a woman who wanted him— and only him—for the rest of her life. But there was one thing he would never do and that was abandon any child of his. Even if he and Gaby didn't work out, they'd be in each other's lives for a long time to come.

The second ADDA SUV drove down the road and parked near the first. Gaby exited the passenger seat and he resisted the urge to run and greet her.

Why she had such an effect over him, he had no idea. They'd known each other hours, yet years of dating and friendship hadn't been enough for his marriage to work.

No. He wouldn't let his ex ruin this. She'd made her

choice, and it was time for Ryan to focus on his own life and happiness.

And for the next three days, it would center around a certain dragonwoman.

Gaby smiled at him as she approached the front door, and he stopped breathing a second. While she'd been pretty inside the hotel, she now had the sunshine highlighting her face and hair, not to mention the green of the trees making her skin come alive. Pretty wasn't a strong enough word. No, she was fucking breathtaking. "Hello, beautiful."

She snorted. "So being outside brings out your charm?"

Grinning, he replied, "I don't know, but something about the fresh air brings it out. Savor it, because it might vanish soon enough."

He winked and she shook her head. "Maybe we can find some sort of middle ground. Otherwise, I'm going to get whiplash."

Ryan ached to reach out and touch her cheek, but he was more than aware of the two ADDA employees watching them. He shouldn't care about them, but for all he knew, Gaby didn't like public displays of affections. And the longer he could go without pissing her off, the better. "Well, let's go inside and I can practice on finding the balance between the two. I know it's in me somewhere."

She opened the door and waved goodbye at the two

cars outside the house. "More than testing your charm, I want some privacy. Come on."

Gaby entered and Ryan followed. As soon as the front door clicked closed, he watched her go about the room and trace first the back of the sofa with her fingers, then a side table, and finally the mantle over the fireplace.

For a woman who helped tame fires and did who knew what other kinds of hard, dangerous work, she had a light touch.

A touch he wanted to feel running along his chest and down to his cock.

And just like that, he was jealous of furniture.

Stop it, Ryan. Geez. He was acting weird for him. He didn't really do jealousy, unless another man was touching his woman when he shouldn't be.

Unless dragon-shifters liked that sort of thing?

Again, he had a steep learning curve ahead of him. Maybe he should've listened to his sister and read more on the topic.

Gaby stopped and faced him, tilting her head to the side. "Well, what do you want to do next?"

Ryan's mind instantly imagined ripping off her clothes and bending her over the couch.

But even if his "task" was to get Gaby pregnant, he wanted her to feel like more than merely a sheath for his cock.

He walked toward her and took her hand. When she wrapped her fingers around his, the awkwardness faded a little. "Tell me something about yourself, something not many people know."

She studied him a second. "Okay, I wasn't expecting that."

Ryan raised his brows. "What? Did you expect me to toss you over my shoulder and carry you upstairs?"

He swore he heard her mutter, "I hope not," but he'd barely processed that before she said in a normal voice, "I think you could since you're strong enough, but let's not." Gaby took a step closer and lightly traced his collarbone over his shirt, the light friction making his heart pound. She continued, "So you want to know something that I don't tell many people?"

Ryan found his voice, which was more gravelly than usual. "Yes, I do."

She studied his gaze, her eyes flashing once, before answering, "As much as I love my family, I have one older brother, my father, four uncles, and seven male cousins who think I can't decide anything for myself, or should at the very least be shielded against even the slightest possibility of danger. They want to control every aspect of my life, all in the name of protecting me. And you know what? I absolutely hate it."

He frowned. "Why would they act that way? You fight fucking fires for a living. I would think that would prove you're tough enough."

She sighed. "They're dragon-shifter males. That's enough of an explanation."

Maybe he should let it drop, caress her cheek, and try

to distract her with his lips. But Ryan sensed this truth of hers was vitally important as to why she'd entered the lottery. Hell, maybe as to why she'd even picked him. "Am I your rebellion, then?"

She never looked away, and he admired her for it. "At first, yes, you were. I thought it'd be nice to be with a human male, someone so different from everything I know."

He studied her face. "I sense a 'but' coming."

She laughed half-heartedly and he yearned to hear a real one. She replied, "But, I don't know. I never expected to want to know you for more than sex, let alone to have this constant hum of attraction to you."

So she felt the pull, too. "So now where does that put us?"

Searching his gaze, she said, "That depends, Ryan Ford. What do you want from this? Tell me now if it's just about sleeping together and leaving. That's completely fine, as that's what we both signed up for. However, if it's more, then tell me. That way I won't try to analyze everything to death."

He decided to be honest, just like she was. "I could bullshit you and say everything would run smoothly and we'd find some sort of magical happy ending. However, it's going to take some time with me when it comes to any woman. I'm definitely a little broken in the relationship and trust depart-ment." He finally cupped her cheek and caressed her soft skin with his thumb. "But I'm starting to think that with you, it may be worth the pain to at least try."

"Then let's try," she murmured.

They stared at one another for a few beats, and yet again, Ryan got the sense that this woman was meant to be his, almost as if he'd been waiting his whole life for her.

Which was crazy, but whenever he tried to dismiss it, it felt wrong.

And for a guy like him, who didn't trust people easily anymore, it was a huge fucking deal. Definitely something he couldn't just push aside and forget about.

Not that he'd reveal all this to the dragon lady anytime soon.

As he stroked her cheek, he loved how she leaned into his touch. He finally spoke again. "I'm more than ready to try, but what are you burning to do first?"

Gaby finally released his hand and leaned against his chest, her heat against him, and her scent invading his senses. He sucked in a breath, and she smiled at the sound. "Well, given all the rules surrounding us for the next three days, maybe we should kiss first and talk later?"

His eyes darted to Gaby's lips. His own throbbed, yearning to caress hers, devour her mouth, to at least make some minor claim on the woman.

He nearly blinked. What was going on with his mind? Ryan wasn't a one-night stand type of guy, let alone so forward.

Yet with Gaby, he couldn't help but be anything but.

She leaned closer and tilted her head upward. She whispered, "So, do you like my suggestion? Because if so, you need to help a girl out with some sort of sign."

His heart racing, he lowered his lips until they were an inch from hers and murmured, "Then I'm going to kiss you, Gabriela Santos, until you can barely breathe."

He closed the distance between them, holding her close against his front, and groaned at the electricity sparking from the contact. He wanted to feel the inside of her mouth, battle her tongue, and then do other wicked things to her body.

Except before he could even work his tongue between her lips, Gaby roared and pushed him away. Dragon-shifters were stronger than humans, even their female ones, and he staggered backward.

Before he could ask anything, Gaby pressed her hands to the sides of her head, closed her eyes, and crouched down into a ball.

Something was wrong.

He moved to check on her, but she growled, "Stay back."

He dared a step, but she opened her eyes, looked right at him with her flashing pupils and stated, "Run, Ryan, unless you want to feel the full force of a dragon in the throes of a frenzy."

"Frenzy?" *Ah, shit.* He vaguely remembered something about that in the binder.

A kiss would let a dragon-shifter know who was their true mate.

And somehow Ryan was Gaby's.

However, as he watched her clenched jaw and her flashing eyes, he couldn't run. For once in his life, a woman needed him—and only him—and he was going to be there for her.

He only hoped he survived the process intact.

So he walked toward her and said, "Bring it on, Gaby. I'm ready for your dragon."

GABY WAS BARELY KEEPING her dragon from taking control of her mind and body.

Even now, her beast thrashed about inside her mind, shouting, *Kiss him, fuck him, claim him. He is* ours *and we need to make sure everyone knows it.*

He needs to make the decision. I won't force him.

Her inner beast roared. *Fate made the decision. He's ours. Claim him before he runs away.*

And that was when Gaby warned Ryan.

But instead of fleeing, he walked toward her and said, "Bring it on, Gaby. I'm ready for your dragon."

Her beast tried harder to take control. *He wants us. Stop fighting it.*

Somehow, she gritted out, "Are you sure? A frenzy is rough and foreign to humans."

He crouched down and touched her cheek. "Yes, I'm sure. Now, tell me what you need, Gaby."

Her dragon finally pushed Gaby to the back of her mind, taking control. Gaby's voice was slightly deeper, signaling it was her beast. "Strip and lay down. I want to fuck you, claim you, and make you mine."

In the next second, her dragon tumbled Ryan to the ground, extended her talons, and ripped off Ryan's clothes.

Gaby watched in horror, wishing her beast would let the human side take him the first time.

Not just his first time with her, but her first time ever with a male, too.

Please, dragon. You can come out again later.

No. You waited too long. I'm claiming our male. Now.

Gaby's dragon shredded their own clothes. Her beast didn't seem to notice how Ryan looked awestruck, as if he'd never seen anything so beautiful.

Oh, Ryan. What I wouldn't give to do this differently, Gaby thought to herself.

Her dragon was already straddling him, positioning his cock at their entrance.

The only good news? He was hard despite being faced with her sex-crazed beast.

He was definitely a strong human.

And yet, Ryan was supposed to be *her* human.

She tried again to push her inner dragon to the back of her mind, but her beast merely created an invisible barrier, trapping Gaby.

From experience, she knew that she wouldn't be able to get out until either her beast grew tired or let her out.

And that made her want to both punch someone and cry.

But as her dragon slammed down on Ryan's cock, uncaring about the twinge of pain at the sudden intrusion, Gaby stopped resisting.

Her dragon had taken her first time from her, and there wasn't anything she could do about it.

As her beast moved their hips, lightly scratching Ryan's chest, Gaby tried hard to enjoy it. But while her dragon didn't care, it hurt a little.

All of this was wrong, so very wrong.

Then Ryan placed his hands on her hips and tried to guide her beast. As he slowed their pace a little, it hurt a little less.

And then his thumb found her clit, brushed in slow circles, and Gaby wanted to gasp at the rush of pleasure.

The rest passed as a blur, their bodies moving, Ryan stoking pleasure, making Gaby want to lean over and kiss him.

However, her dragon only cared about making him come, stealing his seed, and trying to conceive.

At least Ryan kept rubbing and lightly pinching her clit, driving Gaby to the point of orgasm.

When the pleasure finally broke and exploded through her body, Ryan soon stilled her hips and groaned, never taking his eyes from hers despite the fact that with her dragon in control, her pupils would be slitted.

As soon as he slumped back to the floor, her dragon stood and growled, "Again."

Sensing this was her chance since her dragon's guard would be lowered a fraction after the orgasm, she growled and charged the invisible barrier.

The next time with Ryan was hers, no matter what it took.

And finally she broke through to the front of her mind. With a roar, she created a mental prison and tossed her beast inside. Since Gaby's version was more complex, it would hold her beast longer.

Not forever, but long enough.

As she stood breathing hard, she looked at Ryan's face. But he stared down at his cock, with a frown.

And that's when she saw it—her virgin's blood on his dick.

He looked at her. "You were a virgin?"

"I, uh, was, yes."

He swore and rose to his feet. Walking slowly toward her, he murmured, "Are you okay? If I'd known…"

She shook her head. "My dragon didn't care, and it still would've happened the same way, regardless of what you'd tried to say or do."

His gaze never moved from hers. "Will she come back or is she done?"

"She'll be back soon. I can only keep her contained for a short while during a mate-claim frenzy."

She wrapped her arms around her chest and looked at the floor, wishing she could instantly jump into Ryan's arms, kiss him, and pretend the last five or ten minutes had never happened.

But the longer she stood there, the more she hurt between her thighs.

It'd all gone so wrong, the ease between them had vanished, and now Gaby wasn't sure how to fix it.

Ryan came close enough to cup her cheek. "Look at me, Gaby." She did, surprised at the kindness reflecting in his eyes. He continued, "How long do we have until she's back?"

"Why? Do you need to call ADDA to pick you up? Because I would totally understand if you wanted to flee."

He growled. "No fucking way I'm leaving now. And not just because you could already become pregnant with my child." He moved an inch closer, his hot breath dancing on her forehead. "If there's enough time, let me help you shower and relax before she comes out again."

Searching his gaze, she blurted, "Why are you taking this all in stride?"

His other hand cupped her other cheek. As his thumbs strummed her skin, she nearly leaned into him for support. He said, "If a true mate walks away from a dragon-shifter, it's not good, right?"

Gaby shook her head. "No."

They'd probably have to lock Gaby up inside a room

until her beast calmed down, or maybe even pump her full of drugs to make her beast silent.

And it could be that way for years, if her human half lost control.

Ryan's deep voice rolled over her, almost like a caress. "Then let me be the man you need, okay? Which means right now, I need to help clean you up and relax. Will you let me?"

The human male was so different from the drag-onmen she knew. Never would they ask her permission every step of the way, let alone walk away if she'd asked them to. And yet, she sensed Ryan would.

She was glad he wanted to stay and not just because fate had decided he was her true mate, either. The more she learned, the more she liked him as a male, too.

Gaby leaned against him, taking comfort from his heat. "Okay, but it has to be quick. My dragon will be out in twenty minutes or so."

He kissed her lips gently, and some of her earlier fire from his touch returned. She opened her mouth and groaned as his tongue found hers, stroking as if he could never get enough of her, licking every inch as if to memorize her taste and form.

When he finally pulled away, Gaby smiled. "That's a much better first kiss."

The corner of his mouth ticked up. "I'm not sure I can ever surpass waking a dragon's frenzied need for sex, but I agree it was much more of you, Gaby, and I want more." He leaned to her ear. "But first, we need to shower and get you relaxed."

He stepped back, took her hand, and walked until they found the master bedroom and bathroom.

Even though her beast rammed against the mental prison, no doubt roaring to get out, Gaby did her best to ignore her.

The next fifteen or twenty minutes were hers and Ryan's, and no one else's.

She wouldn't constantly fight her dragon during the frenzy as that would only exhaust both female and beast. However, she wanted a little bit more of Ryan's tenderness to balance out her dragon's first rough fucking.

And as he turned on the water and then smiled at her, mischief and heat dancing in his eyes, Gaby did her best to reinforce the mental prison. Maybe she could even have half an hour with her human, if she tried hard enough.

Chapter Four

A mixture of guilt and regret churned inside Ryan as he led Gaby to the shower.

She'd been a virgin, of all things. She sure as hell deserved more than a rough pistoning of hips for her first time. Thank fuck she'd at least orgasmed, or he would've been even angrier with himself.

But the first time with her dragon was over and he couldn't change the past. Besides, if that was the worst her dragon could dish out, he could handle it. Going forward, he'd make sure her inner dragon understood he wanted both of them, not just the beast. He instinctively knew that setting boundaries would be extremely important if he wanted a future with Gaby.

Which he did, despite all the reasons he shouldn't be so sure of it.

As the hot water hit his shoulders and then hers, Gaby moaned and turned to face the spray.

The water cascading down her face, her neck, and the slopes of her breasts made him want to lean in and lick her body all over until she squirmed, begging for him, any pain long forgotten.

However, he didn't have an infinite amount of time with Gaby's human side. Her dragon would return soon enough, so he'd have to make the minutes count and rush a little more than he would if there was no time limit.

As she stood there, he grabbed a bar of soap and reached around her, whispering into her ear, "Ready for the best shower of your life?"

She smiled, but kept her eyes closed. "Someone's a little cocky."

He nipped her earlobe and loved how she sucked in a breath. "I think you'll agree with me soon enough."

Ryan started at her chest, lightly moving the soap down to her breast, taking extra care to swirl around her nipple without touching it. The peak grew tighter, and his mouth watered to taste it.

Soon, Ryan. Soon.

He moved to her other breast and repeated the action, loving how she leaned back, her soft ass cushioning his already hard again dick.

He murmured, "When I have time, I'm going to replace the soap bar with my tongue." He moved it between her breasts, down to her belly, stopping just above her trimmed thatch of dark hair. "Would you like that?"

She moved her hips upward, as if wanting him to touch her lower. "Yes."

"Good." He lightly washed between her legs, being as gentle as he could before he crouched down and continued slowly down her legs, until he reached her ankle. When he finished the other leg, ending at her inner thigh, he spoke again. "Turn for me, Gaby?"

Without hesitation she did, putting his face right at the same level as her pussy.

While his mouth watered to taste her, he continued washing the back of her legs, slowly taking his time with each of her ass cheeks, and then stood to finish up her back and down each arm.

She stared up at him, her pupils still round but slightly dilated, and she said, "Kiss me again, Ryan."

Tossing the soap to the holder, he crushed her against his body and took her lips, instantly delving between them to groan at her hot, sweet taste.

When she clutched his shoulders, he took the kiss deeper, stroking, licking, letting the dragon lady in front of him know he wanted her more than he'd ever wanted anyone in his life. Almost as if he'd burn up if he didn't get to kiss her every day.

After a few minutes, he finally pulled away. Her hot, heavy breaths against his face stirring up his sense of male satisfaction. He said, "There's so much more I want to do with you, Gaby."

"Such as what?"

"While I know it doesn't help the ultimate goal of

getting you pregnant," he paused, moving to her ear and lowering his voice, "I want to lick between those pretty thighs and make you forget about anything but right here, right now, and how much I want you."

Her breath hitched. She surprised him by answering, "I want that, too."

With a growl he lifted her and turned, placing her on the small bench inside the shower.

After giving her one quick kiss, he licked and nibbled his way down her neck, kissed each of her breasts before lightly suckling her hard, pretty nipples, and then continued until he was right in front of her core. He pressed against her thighs and she opened them wider.

Fuck. She was so wet and swollen already, as anxious to have his tongue on her as he wanted to be.

Lowering down, he licked her slit once, loving how she jumped. So he did it again.

Gaby threaded her fingers through his hair, as if telling him he'd better not think of stopping.

So he settled in, licking, lapping, devouring her pussy, groaning at how fucking good her sweet honey tasted. He could lap at her for hours and still not get his fill.

Soon Gaby squirmed, and he licked upward to her clit, careful to circle the hard bud without touching it. He murmured, "Now it's time to really make you love my mouth."

He suckled her clit, lightly flicking it with his tongue, and Gaby arched up toward his head.

He changed to gently biting her, and she screamed in pleasure.

Ryan continued to tease her, licking, nibbling, and even biting until Gaby was moaning about how she was close.

Even though he burned to add a finger or two to her pussy, he resisted. He wanted nothing but for her to feel good and he wouldn't risk hurting her so soon again.

Gaby finally dug her nails into his scalp and arched her back as she came. Just the sound of her short gasps, letting him know she'd orgasmed, made his own dick let out a drop of precum.

His dragon lady finally relaxed back against the wall. Ryan kissed each of her thighs before doing the same up her body until he could meet her gaze. At the lingering pleasure haze in her eyes, he couldn't stop himself from leaning in and taking her lips in a slow, rough kiss.

Gaby finally pulled away and cupped one of his cheeks. She smiled slowly. "I think I could get used to that."

"Me too, Gaby. Me too." After brushing some of her wet hair off her face, he added, "Let's finish up before your dragon comes out again. Otherwise, she might get a little aggressive and send me flying backward onto the tile floor. I'm all for rough sex, but preferably not the kind that could give me a concussion."

He moved to stand, but Gaby took his hand. "Before she comes out, will you have sex with me, Ryan?"

He searched her gaze. While his dick shouted yes, he

didn't want to hurt her. One orgasm didn't make up for the way he'd claimed her virginity. "Are you sure? If you need to rest, I understand."

She stood and placed a hand on his chest. As she lightly traced shapes on his skin, even more blood rushed south. She answered, "Yes. This can be my first time. Before was my dragon's, but now it's my turn."

Damn, he loved that she asked for what she wanted, without embarrassment. He kissed her quickly and turned off the water. "Then let's hurry. I won't take you in the shower for your first time." He winked. "I'll save that for later, when you can handle me being a little rough."

She snorted. "I thought being near tile was a concussion danger zone, or something?"

His eyes turned heated. "Not if I'm in charge, your dragon is contained, and I'm taking you against the wall."

"Oh," she murmured.

Grabbing a towel, he quickly dried her off and then himself. Without another word, he scooped her up and exited the bathroom. She stated, "I can walk, you know."

"Of course you can. But let me show a little strength to try and impress my dragonwoman. I can handle you being stronger than me, but not by much."

She caressed his bicep. "Oh, I know. And eventually, I'll lick every one of your muscles, too."

His cock let out another drop of moisture.

He had no idea how Gabriela Santos knew exactly the right thing to turn him on, but she did. Every time.

Laying her on the bed, he crawled over her. "Ready, my lady?"

She smiled. "Why yes, my dear knight." She lowered her voice. "Just don't try to kill the dragon, okay?"

He chuckled and leaned down, closer to her lips. "Never. I need you in one piece."

His mind added, *For many years to come.*

Pushing aside where the hell that had come from, he closed the distance and took Gaby's lips again.

Not for the first time, Gaby was glad her true mate was human and not a dragon-shifter.

If she had kissed a dragon-shifter true mate, then they'd still be going at it, at the whimsy of one beast or the other, both of them probably unable to control their dragons long enough to do what had just happened in the shower.

Never had Gaby imagined a simple shower being so damn erotic.

Ryan may be a little more considerate than she'd expected, but holy hell, he knew how to use his tongue and make her scream.

And as he framed her body, on his hands and knees above her on the bed, she burned to have him inside her. Any lingering pain be damned.

Then he kissed her, and Gaby reached up to pull him down, loving the feel of his weight and heat over her.

She consciously parted her legs farther, loving how his hard dick pressed against her belly. It took everything she had not to raise her hips and beg.

Not just because she pulsed between her thighs, either. Her dragon had stopped fighting, almost as if she would stay calm as long as they were having sex.

Which suited Gaby just fine. This was her first time, not her dragon's.

Ryan released her lips and kissed her forehead, her cheek, her jaw, and the side of her neck before murmuring, "Why does it feel as if I could never get enough of you? Do you have some sort of spell over me?"

She ran her hands down his back until she could grip his muscled ass in her hands. "No, dragons don't have magical powers or special pheromones. Those are all silly rumors, probably started by dragon groupies to explain their behavior."

Ryan lightly bit where her shoulder met her neck, and Gaby arched her back, loving how her hard nipples pressed against his firm chest.

He moved down, flicking his tongue against her nipple. "I almost want to call you a liar, but I'll just put it up to you being the woman I was waiting for this whole time."

She was aware—just barely, as she had trouble breathing whenever Ryan flicked her nipple with his tongue—how it was probably just the sex making him say that, but she didn't care. "Then show me just how much you want that kind of female, the one meant for you."

His hand snaked down to between her thighs. As he stroked her opening, she parted her legs even more, loving his long fingers against her most sensitive flesh. He growled. "You're so fucking wet already."

"For you, Ryan. I want you."

He gently pressed a finger inside her. While she vaguely recognized some soreness, the more he gently thrust, the harder it was to recognize anything but how good it felt.

And to think, she'd waited so damn long for this kind of closeness. Her make-out sessions had never included penetration of any sort.

Ryan added a second finger, kissing her as he did so, to the point Gaby moved her hips to get him even deeper inside her.

Yes, this is what sex was supposed to feel like. Needing, aching, and a building pleasure that would send her over the edge.

Ryan finally removed his fingers and placed his cock at her center. He deepened his kiss, stroking her tongue, letting her know how much he wanted her.

Gaby pressed against his hard ass, urging him to enter. She wanted—no, needed—to have him inside her or she'd burst.

Inch by slow inch, he filled her, loving how he let her relish the fullness, getting used to him. It still hurt a little, but she hid it. Because no way in hell did she want Ryan to stop now.

When he finally was inside to the hilt, he kissed her

again at the same time his thumb brushed against her clit. She moaned into his mouth and he kept up the torture of both his tongue in her mouth and his thumb on her clit.

Soon she arched her hips, wanting more, done with him staying still. She broke the kiss and said, "Move, Ryan. I need you to move."

To accentuate her words, she arched her hips and clenched her inner muscles. Ryan sucked in a breath. "Fuck, Gaby, I'm not going to last if you do that too much more."

She squeezed him again. "Then start moving or I'll keep teasing you."

With a growl, his hips pulled back and thrust forward slowly, all the while never stopping his thumb on her sensitive bundle of nerves. Between his cock and his wicked caresses, Gaby felt only pleasure and no pain.

But she needed to be a part of it, too, and so she moved her hips to meet his, loving how it made him reach a little deeper inside her, stroking her need even more.

Ryan continued the motion of his hips, his pace increasing with each thrust, and Gaby dug her nails into his ass, careful not to accidentally extend a talon.

Her human male was many things, but he would never heal as quickly as a dragon-shifter. And she needed him in one piece to face her dragon again.

Said male took her lips again, almost as if he needed to feel as much of her heat as possible.

Each motion made the pressure build more, making her skin burn in a good way, and both woman and dragon wanting the pleasure that was so, so close.

Her male never let her up for air and he claimed her mouth and core. Her clit throbbed, needing more than just a light stroking. And as if reading her mind, Ryan pressed down on her clit and she screamed into his mouth, pleasure erupting into her body, sending her into a kind of euphoria where she almost felt like she was floating.

Ryan gave one final thrust and stilled, his tongue still tangling with hers as he groaned and joined her.

When he finally finished, he released her mouth and collapsed on top of her, laying his head on her shoulder.

Both of them breathed heavily, trying to catch their breaths. Her first time with Ryan was such a contrast to that of her dragon's. They hadn't merely fucked. No, it'd felt more like making love.

Not that love was on the table.

Yet.

Although for the first time, Gaby was starting to think maybe fate had picked the right male for her after all.

She lifted a hand to his head and lightly ran her fingers through his hair. She blurted, "That was good, really good."

He looked up at her, those dangerously sexy hazel eyes making her want to claim him all over again. "So it ranked up to your expectation of your own first time?"

Moving her fingers, she traced his jaw, loving the slight stubble there. "And then some."

Ryan took her other hand and threaded his fingers through hers. "I don't want to hurt you again, Gaby. But I can't stop your dragon, once she comes out again."

"I know." She squeezed his hand. "But I think it'll be okay now. And besides, the sooner I'm pregnant, the sooner we can maybe have an actual conversation."

He chuckled. "So you do want me for more than my cock, huh?"

A possessiveness coursed through her—one she'd never felt before. "Yes."

At the fierceness of her words, he sat up a little to better see her face before he said, "I want you to know right here, right now, that no matter what happens in the coming days—weeks?—I will be around to help raise our kid."

Gaby wanted more than a sense of duty, but knew it was soon, way too soon to expect anything else from him.

Still, she couldn't help but tease, "You'll just have to survive my family first. Because if you can't handle them, then you don't stand a chance with our kid."

Just saying "our kid" made her belly flip in a good way.

Ryan raised his brows. "Trust me, if I can deal with my sister, I can deal with anyone."

She snorted. "You may think so, but my family is close, really close, and it's not unusual to have twenty or thirty people at my parents' house for dinner. And subtlety is not an art form that either the Santos or Garcia families are known for."

The corner of his mouth kicked up. "Well, that's a lot different than what the TV is always saying about dragon-shifters being private and almost hermit-like. The more I learn, the more I think you're a lot like humans."

She lightly bopped his nose. "Except for the small detail of us being able to shift into dragons."

He moved up until his face was a few inches from hers. "And I can't wait to see yours. I'm sure you're the prettiest dragon, too, even if I don't know what color she is."

"Gold." The compliment stirred Gaby's beast and she knew it wouldn't be long before her dragon came out and took control again. So she added quickly, "I see you're already trying to get on my dragon's good side. And before she comes out again, I'll let you know that usually she's my best friend and would never try to hurt me. However, the frenzy does things to our inner beasts, things they can't control, either." She bit her lip and said, "If you can find a way to win her over, too, then it might help in the long run."

He cupped her cheek. "I'll try, but ADDA doesn't exactly hand out how-to books when it comes to wooing a dragon."

"You seem resourceful. I'm sure you'll figure it out. Although two small tips—she loves compliments and dirty sex. So, really, when with her, do your worst. She'll love it."

"Well, then, I guess I'll have to get creative."

As he smiled at her, she admired how brave he was. She didn't think many human males would take a mate-claim frenzied dragon so easily.

Speaking of her beast, she stirred inside the mental prison again. So Gaby closed the distance between her and Ryan, needing to kiss him for as long as she could before her dragon broke free.

Ryan pulled her close, into his lap, and tilted her head for better access. She moaned, wishing she could have him make love to her again.

However, the pounding inside her mind grew, to the point she knew her dragon would burst free any second. So Gaby broke the kiss to say, "She's coming, Ryan. Get ready," before her beast took charge of their mind and jumped their human again without warning. A little less frenzied than before, but not by much.

Still, her human male managed to handle her beast almost as well as he had her human side.

And it made her want to get to know him all the more.

Weird as it was to think it, she couldn't get pregnant fast enough. Only then would she regain control and be able to finally date the father of her child.

Chapter Five

D ays and days later—Ryan had lost count after about day five—he awoke, feeling every twinge in his body.

He loved sex as much as the next guy, but a sex marathon was a lot more work than anyone realized.

It was a miracle he didn't have cock burns by this point.

But then he looked over, finding Gaby awake and smiling at him, and her smile erased every ache in his body. He rolled over to cup her cheek and kiss her gently. "Good morning, I think?"

"Yes, it's still morning, but only just."

She studied him a second and only the smile on her face prevented him from worrying. "What is it?"

"Well, I don't know how else to put this, but it's happened. My dragon suspected, and the special pregnancy test confirmed it—we're having a baby."

He blinked as she took his hand and placed it over her lower belly. Ryan stared at their hands, fully aware that had been the goal, but this was reality.

As long as everything went right, he'd be a father in about nine months' time.

With a whoop, he rolled Gaby to her back and kissed her, slipping his tongue into her mouth and stroking hers slowly, possessively, letting her know he wanted all of this. The baby, them being parents, and him with her.

Well, maybe the last part wasn't settled yet, but he was going to work on it.

He finally let them both up for air and Gaby searched his eyes. "So you're still happy about this, huh?"

"Happy? Baby, that doesn't even begin to describe what I'm feeling. This will be our adventure, one that's going to last a long, long time."

She moved a hand to his hair and lightly played with it. He wanted to lean into her touch but didn't dare break his gaze with the mother of his child.

The woman he wanted to be his wife, if she'd let him.

Wait, wife? Ryan expected panic to set in at the word, but only a sense of rightness settled over him. He had a feeling that if fate had said she was his mate, then he'd have a good chance with her, better than he'd had before.

So now his plan included wooing and wedding his dragon lady.

Gaby kissed his cheek and then tried to roll away. However, Ryan held her close, asking, "Do we really have to leave this bed yet?"

She snorted. "After being in this bed nonstop for about ten days, you want to stay some more?"

He brushed hair away from her cheek. "I just want some time with you, Gabriela Santos. As much as I've come to like your dragon, I want some time alone with your human side."

"Well, I could wait an hour or two before calling ADDA and my clan." She raised her brows. "Although fair warning—I want food above sex right now."

He grinned. "Well, it's a good thing I can make a mean bacon and eggs. If there's any downstairs, that is. It's not like we've had a lot of time to check out the fridge."

She laughed, and his good mood went even higher. She said, "I'm not sure, but let's go find out? I hope there's more than ketchup and moldy cheese, though."

She slipped out from under him, grabbed a robe, and raced out of the room.

Oh, she wanted to play chase, did she? Ryan ran after her, snagging his boxers and tugging them on along the way. He caught up with her at the bottom of the stairs and hauled her back against his front. As he nuzzled her cheek, he murmured, "Gotcha."

She giggled, and the sound made him grin. Gaby said, "I let you catch me."

"Did you now?"

She looked over her shoulder, to meet his gaze. "Dragon-shifters can run faster than most humans, and I'm not just any dragon-shifter. Part of my job requires lots of drills and training. You don't stand a chance against me, human."

He hugged her tighter against his chest. "Once we're both rested, we may need to put that statement of yours to the test. Being a programmer may not require as much physical training as your job, but I've spent a lot of time in my home gym over the last two years. I may beat you yet."

She tilted her head and tapped her chin. "Hm, if you're nice to me, I might even give you a head start and then maybe you'll have a chance to best me."

He twirled her around and placed one hand on her ass and the other on the nape of her neck. "We'll see, Gaby. I may surprise you."

She sucked in a breath, her pupils flashing, right before she wiggled out of his hold—making his cock more than ready again—and dashed toward the kitchen.

Chuckling, he went after her, hoping he'd get more than an hour alone with his dragon lady. He wanted more, so much more.

GABY RUSHED into the kitchen and dashed to the far side of the island in the center. Seconds later, Ryan entered and headed toward her.

She could probably evade him indefinitely if she really wanted, but both woman and beast craved the will-he-or-won't-he chase.

Her human may never be able to follow her into the air, but as he circled and mirrored her actions around the kitchen island, she didn't care.

This, right here, was what she'd always wanted. A male who was sexy as hell in bed but also playful out of it.

The only thing left was to see if he could stand up to her family and the others on PineRock.

Normally her dragon would pipe up with an opinion, but her inner beast was too tired to say anything. But Gaby didn't worry. Frenzies tended to wear dragons out and make them a little more complacent for a few days after, or so her brother had said.

Not wanting to think about her brother and allow reality to invade quite yet, she darted in the opposite direction, straight for Ryan. She jumped into his arms and he caught her, hugging her against his body. He grinned as he said, "Giving up while you still can, darling?"

Looping her arms around his neck, she grinned back. "You can think that way, if it helps to stroke your ego. But one day you'll see me at full force, I'll win, and then I'm going to collect a prize from you."

"A prize, huh?" He nuzzled her cheek. "I'm not enough of a prize?"

She leaned into his caress. "You're a great prize, but competition and small bets make things more interesting."

He leaned back to look into her eyes. At the amusement in his gaze, she wanted to jump onto the counter and ask him to take her all over again.

But she resisted. They'd had plenty of sex over the last week and a half. For now, she wanted to know him a little better before he met her clan, but especially her family. Everyone would either want to talk, observe, or challenge him at first.

Days could go by before Gaby could have more than an hour or two alone with her human.

Ryan kissed her, banishing her worries about the near future, and eventually set her back on her feet. "Speaking of bets, do I remember right that Vegas has 'no dragon-shifter gambling allowed' signs all over the city?"

She sighed. "You remember right, they do. However, Reno will let us enter a few of their casinos. And that's only because the dragon clans help with emergencies in the city sometimes, when humans can't quite handle it themselves."

He brushed the hair off her cheeks. Would she ever tire of his warm, strong fingers against her skin?

He did it again, and she decided, nope.

Ryan grunted. "Well, at some point we're going to visit one of those casinos in Reno then. Because I'd like to take my dragon lady out on the town before the baby comes."

The baby. Even though she'd stared at the special pregnancy test herself—one used only for dragon-shifters to detect early conception—for about five minutes, it still seemed unreal.

But as she stared at the handsome, grinning man above her, she knew that as long as he was around to help, it would turn out okay.

Well, as long as everything went smoothly once she returned to Clan PineRock with him. He *was* only human after all, which made him an easy target.

Her dragon said groggily, *If anyone tries to hurt him, we'll protect him.*

I know, dragon. I just wish we didn't have to worry about it.

Before Ryan could ask her about her flashing eyes and her dragon, she wanted to keep their conversation light and said, "I'd like that. I'm not much of a gambler myself. I deal enough with high stakes for my job, but there are shows and even games and things in Reno. I think Circus Circus is one of the casinos who'll let me inside, and there's plenty to do there."

He chuckled. "Whatever my lady wishes, we'll do. Except I want to take one of those cheesy commemorative photos they have at some casinos with you, and more than once, too."

"I think we can manage that, although you have heard of cell phones, right? And a selfie?"

He rolled his eyes. "I'm not *that* old, Gaby."

When he lightly smacked her ass, she laughed. "Okay, okay. But I can't make any promises about not teasing you later, though."

Her belly rumbled, which made Ryan frown. "Let's get you something to eat, darling. Okay?"

She nearly sighed at his lovely twang. She'd never get tired of it.

Even though he released her body, he took her hand in his to walk to the fridge.

Her heart warmed at the gesture. Even after everything, he still constantly wanted to touch her.

And her possessive dragon side reveled in it.

After scouting the contents of the fridge, Ryan stated, "I guess it's going to be toast, eggs, and yogurt. There's not much else left in here."

The ADDA employees had been leaving groceries at the front door every few days, not that Gaby could remember what she'd eaten most of the last two weeks. "It's food, which is all that matters."

Even though he released her hand, he motioned around his waist. "Hold me from behind. That way we can talk while I cook."

It would be easier for her to pull up a chair near the stove, but she craved the closeness too much.

So Gaby complied, and followed him to the stove and nearby counter. As he prepped things, she said, "I never heard much about your sister, aside from the fact she got you to enter the dragon lottery. And since it would've been weird to bring her up during the frenzy, will you tell me about her now?"

Even though she had her head against his back, she could hear the smile in his voice. "Tiffany is a lot younger than me, by about ten years. She was a surprise for my parents, but I'm glad she's around. I'm not sure I would've survived the last two years without her."

Because of his bitchy ex-wife. True, Gaby didn't know a whole hell of a lot about her, but the fact she'd cheated and married Ryan's twin was enough to anger both woman and beast. "Why, what did she do to help you?"

"Well, she never let me hide away from the world too long, and continually tried to get me to do something, anything, outside of my house." He turned on a burner, placed the frying pan, and continued. "I even started working from home to avoid everyone, and the results weren't pretty. Let's just say I'm glad she never gave up on me. If she had, I wouldn't be here now."

He touched one of her arms around his waist and she hugged him tighter. "I hope she can visit soon. I'd like to meet her."

He snorted. "Oh, she'll visit. I don't think you could stop her, if I'm honest. Tiffany is sort of awed by dragon-shifters in general."

The rules were different for the human entrants, in that not all siblings had to enter at the same time to qualify. So she asked, "But she didn't enter the lottery for herself?"

Ryan shook his head. "No. She wanted to make sure I was okay first."

There was a hint of guilt in his voice. Gaby released him to stand at his side. Only when he met her gaze did she say, "Well, you are now, right?" He gave a small nod and she added, "Then maybe I can help your sister. While I can't rig the lottery, she can at least visit Pine-Rock. I have plenty of single cousins, after all. If she wanted to enter the lottery, I guess she likes men?" Ryan nodded again. "Then there are a lot more options for her, given how dragon-shifters skew male."

Ryan sighed. "Please don't tell her about your plethora of single cousins or she'll stop at nothing to nab one."

Gaby shrugged. "It wouldn't be that bad, provided she doesn't mind overprotectiveness."

Ryan gave a half-laugh. "Having two, much-older brothers during her teen years wasn't easy, so I'm sure she can handle herself. Not that I'm encouraging it, mind you."

She leaned against his arm, watching him stir the eggs into the pan. Gaby burned to ask about Ryan's twin, yet she didn't want to ruin the morning.

No, she'd ask later, once they'd spent more time together.

Once the eggs were cooking, Ryan popped some bread into the toaster and glanced at her. "Right now, I probably should be more worried about your brother and that gaggle of male relatives you talked about."

The term gaggle made her think of them with feathered wings instead of normal dragon ones, and she laughed. "I dare you to call them a gaggle to their faces."

"Not if I want to stay alive, darling. I'd prefer they

didn't change into dragons and drop me from a great height."

She lightly hit his side. "They won't do that. Although they'll threaten it, I'm sure. But me and my cousin Luna are the only female cousins in the family, and they'd all do anything to protect us, which should soon extend to you, too."

Ryan stirred the scrambled eggs again. "Well, if you have any hints on how to get into their good graces, now would be a great time to tell me. After all, we'll be on your clan later today."

Yes, they would. What she wouldn't give for another day alone with Ryan.

However, if ADDA found out they'd been keeping the pregnancy secret, the contract spelled out consequences.

In other words, ADDA wanted to wash their hands of them as soon as possible.

She glanced up at Ryan's expectant face. "Just don't act afraid and you'll do fine, I think. Fear will make you unworthy in their eyes. And even though it's my life and my decisions, some of them will ignore that and think you need their approval before you can be with me. The only good news is that my brother has a human mate now, so at least you'll have an ally."

It had hurt a little to receive the text message from Jose about his mating ceremony, but she couldn't fault him for wanting everything legal, to give his mate the best protection under the law.

Her dragon sniffed. *We've met Tori and like her. That's all that matters.*

Breakfast ready, Ryan divvied up the eggs, took the bread out of the toaster, and dished out the yogurt. Taking both plates, he put them on the island behind them.

He, of course, put the plates really close together.

When she raised her brows, he said, "I was thinking you could sit in my lap."

She snorted. "Right, because that won't lead to other things."

He crossed his heart. "I promise you'll keep your robe on."

She shook her head. But after he sat, she jumped into his lap and leaned against his chest. "I'm feeding myself, though. And that's not up for discussion."

"Ah, and here I thought to 'accidentally' miss your mouth and get yogurt on your lips. Which then I'd have to lick clean, of course."

She lightly hit his chest but grinned as she did it. "Are you sure you're not part dragon-shifter?"

"Since I can't shift, nope, I'm not. Just a guy wanting to be as close as possible to his woman."

Maybe it should bristle her feathers—it probably would've coming from anyone else—but she liked being "his woman."

Putting a finger into the yogurt, she dabbed it on his lips. "Well, look at that. I guess I'll need to keep my male clean, huh?"

He grinned, but lowered his head down, not quite touching her lips. Gaby licked once, twice, three times until the yogurt was gone.

But to tease him, she stayed where she was and didn't close the distance between their lips.

Ryan growled. "Woman, you drive me crazy."

"That's the plan."

With another growl, he kissed her and held her tighter against his body. Gaby immediately parted her lips, loving his strong tongue against hers, branding his taste with her own.

All too soon, he pulled away. "Eat, love. You need food more than kisses right now."

As if conspiring with him, her belly rumbled.

With a sigh, she picked up her plate and fork. "I used to like eating, but now it just irritates me because it's stealing time away from our happy bubble."

"I want this happy bubble to last a long, long time, Gaby. Possibly forever. So enjoy your meal and know I want to have this every day with you, no matter where we are."

She paused with the fork partway to her mouth as her heart skipped a beat.

Gaby wanted that, too. And if he kept it up, she'd be in love with him in a matter of weeks, if not days.

Not yet, Gaby. Since he was a human male, he didn't have to live on PineRock after getting her pregnant. He could leave at any time.

And so she needed to ensure he wanted to stay, root

up his entire life, and be with her forever before any mention of love or feelings.

So she ate her breakfast, talking about nothing and everything with her human, and hoped her clan would welcome the male into their fold.

Chapter Six

L ater the same day, Ryan sat next to Gaby inside an
SUV, with his arm around her shoulders. He'd lost
track of how long they'd driven by mountains, pine trees,
and various forms of water, but he finally spotted a huge
metal gate covering some kind of tunnel up ahead.

Gaby murmured, "That's the entrance to PineRock."

The gate opened and as they drove through the
tunnel, Gaby leaned against his side. He wanted to stare
down at her face, to memorize the last few moments they
had nearly alone, but as they exited the tunnel, he
couldn't tear his gaze from a giant black dragon
launching into the sky, joining another purple one
hovering in the air, waiting for their friend.

"Damn, they're big," he whispered.

Gaby laughed. "Those are two females. Males are
even bigger."

He frowned and finally tore his gaze from the two

dragons soaring away from the surrounding mountains. "Great. So that's what I have to contend with, times how many men in your family?"

"Only thirteen adult males. I have a second cousin who's too young still, so that's one less worry."

"Gaby," he growled.

She grinned. "Oh, come on, this is fun." Her expression turned serious. "I can tease you. However, if my family does, they'll have to deal with me."

He played with a section of her hair. "I hope you'll let me try to handle them first."

The ADDA employee driving the car, Ashley, snorted. "Good luck with that. It took me about three years on the job to finally meet them head-to-head without flinching."

Gaby growled, "You're not helping, Ashley."

The woman replied, "Hey, it's the truth, and I find that helps the most when it comes to humans and dragon-shifters. And since I'll be watching over Ryan—in addition to your new sister-in-law, Tori—you'll just have to put up with me and my ways, Gaby."

Ryan chimed in. "It'll be fine. And honesty is always the best policy, even when it's bad news." He touched Gaby's cheek with his free hand, until she looked at him again. "Just give me a chance with your relatives before coming to my defense, okay? You mentioned how they like strength, and I want to show them I have it, especially beyond just the physical."

Gaby sighed. "You know what? I just realized that I

sound like all my overprotective male cousins, and I really don't want to. So yep, try away. But I'll always have your back, Ryan. So don't be afraid to ask for my help. They can, after all, change into giant dragons."

He lightly pinched her side. "I'll keep that in mind, minx."

She grinned and Ryan's heart skipped a beat. Yes, for this woman he'd face an army of dragons and find a way to come out the other side in one piece.

Ashley pulled in front of a nondescript building several stories tall and shut off the engine. Turning in her seat, she glanced between them. "I waited to tell you this until we were here, so you wouldn't get nervous. But while you two were away, someone attacked Jose and Tori's cabin."

Gaby's brother and his wife. Gaby leaned forward and Ryan did, too. Gaby said, "Tell me they're okay, and the baby, too."

Ashley waved a dismissive hand in the air. "They're both unharmed, although a little shaken. The reason I bring it up now instead of letting your clan leader tell you is that both of you need to be on your guard from the second you step out of this car. While Wes has started to clean house, he thinks there may be a few lingering clan members who are pretending to accept humans living on PineRock, but in truth, they're lying in wait to try and attack again."

Ryan tightened his grip on Gaby's shoulder. "I hope the clan leader can tell us how to spot them, apart from the obvious, such as when one attacks me. Or, at the very least, he should give me some tips on how to protect against them."

Ashly nodded. "Wes and his head Protector, Cris, will have plenty to say to you. But since no one can hear anything said in this car—ADDA decided to take precautions in light of recent events—I want to add that it's possible even one of the Protectors could be suspect at this point. So trust Gaby's family, Cris, Wes, and the head doctor, Troy Carter. The rest we'll have to watch and be vigilant about."

Gaby unconsciously put a hand over her belly and murmured, "Not the best atmosphere to have a half-dragon-shifter child, is it?"

Ryan leaned closer to his woman and said, "Whatever needs doing, I'll help. I won't allow any child or woman of mine to come to harm if I can help it."

Gaby smiled weakly at him. "Let's hope the worst is over."

Ashley cleared her throat. "Probably, but regardless, given everything Wes, Cris, and ADDA are doing, things should be figured out in no time." She gestured toward the building. "Now, let's get going. If we're late, I'll never hear the end of it."

Once he and Gaby disembarked, Ryan drew her against his side and rubbed her upper arm.

He'd known there would be challenges, but it seemed as if he'd be facing them from day one instead of some later date.

However, he hadn't been bluffing—he'd do whatever it took to protect his child and hopefully future wife. Sure, he was at a huge disadvantage being human, but there had to be some way—or ways—for him to protect his soon-to-be family.

And even if it took him training every day until he fell dead from sleep, it was a small price to pay for the future he wanted so desperately.

GABY WALKED down the corridor of the main clan security building, her head buzzing, and tried her best not to give everyone the side-eye.

She'd always thought PineRock was a relatively peaceful place, one that didn't suffer some of the extreme hatred and prejudices of other dragon clans in the US.

But it seemed even her beloved home had its share of bad apples.

Her dragon spoke up. *I trust Wes and Cris. They'll make it a safe space. Until then, we'll just have to be careful.*

She glanced at Ryan from the corner of her eye. *I wonder if ADDA will even let him stay now. Tori is legally mated to my brother, so there's no danger there of them sending her away. Ryan isn't similarly protected.*

Her beast fell silent, no doubt because it wasn't as easy for a female dragon-shifter to mate a human male. One major reason was some old-fashioned bullshit about how a male dragon-shifter could protect their human female mate, but a female dragon-shifter wouldn't be able to accomplish the same for her human male.

Gaby kept up with all the male dragons in her fire-fighting unit. Even against a male dragon bigger than her, she could hold her own.

But even if she convinced ADDA of that, the problem ran deeper. After all, Ryan had fulfilled his lottery contract requirement—she was pregnant. And ADDA didn't see a reason to create more trouble and paperwork by letting human males stay. Neither of the males from the last two lotteries had been allowed to live permanently with the dragon clans. Something about them not being dedicated enough.

Of course they couldn't use the dedicated reasoning with Ryan. Her human was dedicated, more than she'd ever dreamed. She had to believe that between her strength and his actions, he'd get to stay with her.

Because if he didn't, Gaby's heart would break. It hadn't been long, but it was enough. She cared for the human and was halfway in love with him, too.

Her dragon growled. *Don't think like that. Otherwise we'll be defeated before we even start.*

I'll try my best. But I won't pretend the odds aren't against us.

They have been from the beginning, but that doesn't mean I'm going to just give up.

I'm not giving up, dragon.

Good.

They arrived at the conference room used for visitors —namely ADDA employees—and Gaby tried her best to push all the negative thoughts away so she could face her clan leader with a clear head.

Ryan never loosened his hold on her shoulders as they entered. The three people sitting at the other side of the long table all stared at them.

The three were Wes Dalton, PineRock's clan leader; Cristina Juarez, their head Protector; and Dr. Troy Carter, their head doctor.

It was Wes, the auburn-haired male in the middle, who snorted. "Calm down, human. None of us are going to steal her away from you."

She felt Ryan relax a fraction at her side. The urge to make a quip was strong, but she held back, to allow Ryan the chance to stand his ground.

Her male replied, "All the same, I'll keep her close."

The woman with light brown skin and dark hair rolled her eyes—Cris. "And to think Gaby always complained about how possessive dragon males are. And now she's gone and found herself a human who's no different."

Gaby growled. "He's not the same at all, and he's mine. So be nice, Cris."

Cris raised her brows. "Well, well, has the male made you snippy or have your pregnancy hormones already kicked in?"

The dark-skinned male with a shaved head, Dr. Carter, looked at Cris with raised brows. "Let's just be grateful it's not you, Cris. If you ever get pregnant, I might just have to take a long vacation and let the junior doctor monitor you. Otherwise, I may not survive the ordeal with my balls intact."

Cris raised her brows. "Who says we have to wait for me to be pregnant? I can gladly rid you of your balls now."

Gaby bit her lip to keep from smiling. All three dragon-shifters sitting together were friends and teased each other endlessly. However, she wasn't sure how it'd all appear to Ryan, though.

Not that she got the chance to check on him because Ashley clapped her hands until she had everyone's attention. "Now, now, children, given all the crap that's happened recently, maybe you can save the bickering for later?"

Wes crossed his arms over his chest and gave the human his best stare.

Not that it affected Ashley one bit.

Wes spoke, dominance threaded into his voice. "I think you've been spending too much time on PineRock, Ms. Swift, and you're starting to forget your place."

Ashley raised her dark eyebrows. "*My* place? Huh. Funny, I thought you were the one who owed me a favor."

Gaby looked between the pair. "Did I miss something?"

Wes grunted. "No, it's just ADDA business." He focused on Gaby and Ryan. "Which brings me to you two. I assume Ms. Swift told you about what happened to Jose and Tori?"

"Only vaguely," Gaby answered.

"Well, you need to hear the full extent to ensure you take this threat seriously." Wes leaned forward. "Two males threw huge stones through the front window of their cabin. If Tori had been in that room, they would've killed her."

Gaby's heart skipped a beat. "Even though she was already pregnant?"

Wes grunted affirmative.

Holy hell, that was bad, really bad.

Ryan asked, "While they shouldn't try to kill anyone, why do I sense that her being pregnant makes it worse?"

Gaby answered, "Dragon-shifters treasure children since we've come close to extinction many times in the past. The thought of killing a pregnant woman is one of the worst things you can do. Which means whoever did it must truly hate humans." She growled, no doubt her pupils flashing at the same time. "Who tried to kill my sister-in-law?"

Cris didn't miss a beat. "The Randalls. And before the human asks, they were transferred to PineRock after a California wildfire destroyed their clan. While it doesn't excuse anything, it at least helps to know they're newer to PineRock. The entire family is now in the hands of ADDA, although both sides are trying to figure out if they influenced others here with their anti-human vitriol."

Wes jumped in. "Exactly. There may still be more individuals, waiting among the thousand or so clan members here, to strike any human who comes to Pine-Rock." He fixed his gaze on Ryan. "Which is why I'm trying to figure out what to do with you."

Gaby frowned. "What does that mean?"

Wes glanced between her and Ryan. "I'm not sure it's safe to keep him here."

She opened her mouth to protest, but Ryan was first. "I'll do whatever it takes to stay, but I'm not leaving Gaby. And before you go on about rules, could you abandon a woman pregnant with your child?"

Wes sighed. "No. And I get it, but I also have to consider your safety. A dead human would look bad for the clan, not to mention for me."

Ashley cleared her throat and everyone looked at her. "I believe the ultimate decision about whether he can stay or not is mine, Wes."

Wes growled out, "Not entirely."

Ashley raised her brows. "Do you need a lecture in protocol?"

As the pair stared at each other, Gaby sensed it could turn into a long, drawn-out argument that would end nowhere.

So Gaby spoke up. "Regardless, the rules say he can visit a few days at a time, if he wishes, at least until the baby is born. This is his first visit, so he doesn't have to leave just yet. And seeing how ADDA loves their contracts, are you really going to risk breaking it, Wes?"

Wes nodded. "I just might."

Her dragon woke from her nap. *I don't like this.*

Neither do I, but don't you want Ryan here?

Of course I do. But not if it means he'll end up dead.

Aware that they were all talking about him without talking to him, Gaby looked up at her human and asked, "What do you want, Ryan? Even with more information now, do you still want to stay if there's a possibility you can end up dead?"

He didn't hesitate. "Yes."

Dr. Carter grunted. "You just went up a few notches in my book, Ford."

Ryan merely shrugged. "I promised Gaby that I'd stay with her as long as I could, and I take promises very seriously."

No doubt in part because of how betrayed he was a couple of years ago, when his ex-wife broke the ultimate promise.

She wanted Ryan safe, but more than before, she wanted to keep him near. He was her human. Hers.

Cris tapped her fingers on the table. "I don't see how him staying a few days will hurt. If we try to send him away before Gaby's family meets him, there will be hell to pay, I'm sure. And I don't need any extra work, if I can help it."

Gaby straightened a little at Cris's words. "That's right. If he's nestled among twenty, or more, of my relatives, then no one would think to try and attack all of us, would they?"

Wes said, "It's possible they still would." She opened her mouth to protest, but he put up a hand and she remained silent. "However, I can at least allow Ryan to stay for a week, to help you get settled before you go back to work. This means you'll accept constant surveillance from a group of Cris's most-trusted Protectors for that week, though. Understood?"

She sensed tension in Ryan, his muscles going stiff. Oops. They really hadn't talked about her going back to work, had they? Not like she'd dive headfirst into a fire or anything, but she could shift until the last trimester of her pregnancy and Gaby planned on helping any way her superiors would allow her.

She'd have to find a way to bring it up again later.

Gaby cleared her throat. "We'll grudgingly accept the Protectors."

"Good," Wes stated. "You'll also have regular check-ins. Not the most convenient thing for a new couple, but I won't budge on that either."

Ryan bobbed his head. "If it means staying, I'll suffer it gladly."

Cris stood. "Then before I coordinate all of that, Ryan and I need to have a little talk."

Gaby was about to say she'd go with him, but Dr. Carter motioned toward Gaby first and said, "Before you go anywhere else, you need to come to the clinic with me, Gaby. If I don't check you out and verify everything's okay, then your parents and brother will probably kill me."

She rolled her eyes. "They would never hurt you. Your sister is mated to one of my cousins, after all."

"All the more reason for me to make doubly sure you're fine." The doctor stood. "Is there anything else you need her for right now, Wes? I have a minor surgery in three hours, and I'd like to squeeze in Gaby's exam first."

Wes also stood. "As long as Ryan stays to go over a few things with Cris, I don't see why we can't all get back to business. However, you two"—he pointed at Gaby and Ryan—"will visit with me privately tomorrow, around lunchtime. We still have other things to discuss."

Anxious to go with Dr. Carter and get that over with so she could introduce Ryan to her family, she nodded. "Fine, fine, we'll be there. Can we go now?"

Wes glanced at Ryan. "Good luck with her, human."

She growled, but Ryan spoke over the sound. "No luck is needed, Mr. Dalton. I'm fortunate to have her, and I'll never take Gaby for granted."

And just like that, her irritation at all the demands and coddling from the last little while faded.

She was a little bit smitten with her male. Just a tad.

Cris nodded in approval. "Good answer. You may yet do okay here."

Dr. Carter headed toward the door. "Then let's go. Oh, and Ford, if you think of any questions related to Gaby's pregnancy, then come and find me. The more information you have, the easier this whole process will be."

Ryan merely squeezed Gaby's shoulder. "Thank you, Dr. Carter. I will."

Wes dismissed them. Gaby lingered back a second

with Ryan, ignoring both Dr. Carter and Cris frowning a few feet away. She murmured, "I'll return as quickly as I can."

He caressed her cheek. "I'll be fine, Gaby. Don't worry about me."

It was hard not to.

However, Ryan gently kissed her, and she fought the urge to take it deeper.

Dragon-shifters weren't usually shy about showing affection, but she wasn't quite ready for Cris and Dr. Carter to watch Ryan fuck her mouth with his tongue.

So she broke the kiss, touched his jaw, and turned to follow the doctor out of the main security building and toward the center of the clan's lands, where the clinic was located.

Well, it was more of a mini-hospital than a clinic, but all American dragon clans just called them clinics.

Regardless, there were more important things to think about. Gaby had one week to convince Wes and the others that Ryan should stay. And not just because her dragon would want their human nearby, either, since that wouldn't be enough of a reason.

But to do that would require a plan and probably the help of her extended family.

She'd often thought of them as a burden when young, but now Gaby appreciated her nosey but loving family. They may just be the shield she needed to keep her human at her side.

Chapter Seven

R yan survived his meeting with the head Protector and even a brief Q&A with the doctor afterward.

The latter had been quite eye opening, with the doctor revealing all the rules for female dragon-shifters and how they became vital to follow as Gaby's pregnancy progressed. Although some of them seemed ridiculous—like not watching any sort of emotional movie during the last month—he had some time to sort through them all and find out if they were indeed necessary.

But for now, he merely walked hand in hand with his lady toward a bright yellow house, one with music drifting from the windows.

It was time to meet her family.

Gaby squeezed his hand. "Don't worry, once you pass their initial questions, everything will be fine. And like I said, win over my mom and it'll make the rest of the process a lot smoother."

He shook his head, smiling. "I'm not worried about your mother. It's more all those male relatives who shift into giant dragons who I'm concerned about." He paused and added, "Although, I wish I could've seen you in your dragon form first. I've never seen a dragon up close, but I reckon that once I do, I won't be as intimidated by the thought of it."

Gaby gave him a sympathetic gaze. "Believe me, my beast wants to preen for you as soon as possible and score some good ear scratches. But being late to dinner would be a fatal first step since my parents think being on time is basically being late." She smiled at him again. "We'll set aside some time for it tomorrow, okay?"

Bringing their clasped hands up, he kissed the back of Gaby's. "It's a date."

Gaby beamed at the words, and his heart skipped a beat. If only he had the power to fast-forward through the evening until tomorrow.

Not happening, he thought to himself. Her family was not only important to her, they would also be helping to protect him.

In other words, he needed her family's approval more than they needed his. That meant being on his best behavior for the evening and digging up any charm he could muster.

They were still about ten feet from the front door when it swung open, revealing the tall, dark-haired form of the man Gaby had shown him in pictures earlier—her older brother, Jose.

Jose studied him, his dark-eyed expression unreadable.

The stare down was probably meant to intimidate him, but Ryan didn't flinch or miss a step. He'd been that older brother for his sister before and understood it was more a test than a real threat.

Especially since Ryan would rather cut off his legs than hurt Gaby.

Jose finally grunted. "So this is him."

Gaby sighed. "I was *much* nicer and friendlier to your human when I first met her. Could you at least try to have some manners with mine?"

He waved at Ryan. "If he wants to have my sister, then he has to earn it."

Gaby growled, but Ryan beat her to it. "Isn't that Gaby's decision to make and not yours?"

For a second, Jose narrowed his eyes at him. But then he snorted. "Maybe now. She was the worst decision maker as a child, though." He shrugged. "Old habits die hard."

Ryan was about to ask for the dragonman to clarify, but Gaby grunted and said, "Don't even start on the embarrassing childhood stories yet, Jose."

Jose raised his brows. "Or, what? Will you torture my ears with awful music?"

Okay, Ryan didn't know what that meant, but he hated being on the outside when it concerned his dragon lady. He'd add the reference to his list of things to ask about.

Gaby smiled sweetly. "I'll leave ear-related torture to our cousin. I'd rather surprise you one morning by maybe plastering pictures of you naked as a child, or dressed up as an old-woman-looking warlock, all over your house. I'm sure the clan would get a good chuckle out of that."

Jose shook his head. "Seeing as Tori and I are staying here at our parents' house right now, I don't think you want to risk Mom's wrath."

A woman's voice cut through. "Smart move, son." An older woman, who was slightly shorter than Jose, with black hair streaked with gray and deep brown eyes, smiled at Ryan. "And you must be Ryan Ford." She gestured to Jose and then Gaby. "I'm the mother of these two troublemakers. Please, call me Maria, Ryan."

Gaby tugged Ryan forward, ignoring her brother, and said, "Tell Jose to be nice for the evening. I behaved for his mate, after all."

Ryan bit his lip to keep from chuckling. Gaby was twenty-four and her brother even older, yet their mother was the peacekeeper.

At one time, his family had been close, too. No longer.

Not wanting to think of the past right now, he cleared his throat and all eyes turned to him. "Nice to meet you, Maria. Is that barbecue I smell? Both Gaby and I could do with some food."

"Why didn't you say so?" Maria moved in between him and Gaby, forcing them apart so she could place a hand on each of their backs. "One big tip, Ryan—keep your pregnant mate fed, or you'll risk a very grumpy dragonwoman."

"Mom," Gaby growled.

Ryan grinned. "Don't worry, we already decided that I was the better cook. Nowhere near what you are, from what I've heard, but good enough."

Maria studied him a second. "You *are* good, human, starting with the compliments early." He winked at Maria, and she laughed before adding, "Then come along. I'm the only one who'll be able to get you to the backyard for some dinner without everyone stopping you along the way."

As the older dragonwoman guided them down a hall and through a few rooms—raising her brows to stop anyone from approaching along the way—Ryan met Gaby's gaze over Maria's head.

She mouthed, "Good job."

The praise made him walk a little taller. So far, so good. He hoped the rest of the night went as smoothly.

GABY HAD EXPERIENCED Ryan's charm firsthand but was still impressed at the way he handled her mother.

Not to mention her brother, who was trailing behind him. Maybe they could bond over being older brothers or something. Gaby said over her shoulder, "Where's Tori?"

Jose frowned. "She wanted some time alone with Luna."

Uh-oh. "That can't be good."

Jose growled. "Luna attracts trouble, sure, but she's one of the few friends Tori's made on PineRock so far and I won't deny her."

She blinked. "Who are you and what have you done with my brother?"

Her mother spoke up. "A mate has done him well. All dragon males like to think they know how they'll handle a female, but usually it's unrealistic."

"So does this mean if we get all the cousins paired off that they'll leave me and Luna alone for good?" Gaby asked.

Her mother shrugged. "It wouldn't hurt, although I'm not sure if their true mates are on PineRock, which makes it difficult."

Gaby whispered, "Ryan has a younger sister."

"Gaby," Ryan growled.

She shrugged. "What? It wouldn't hurt for them to at least meet her. Besides, my mom here will want to meet her, too."

Her mother clicked her tongue. "Eventually, yes. But not until we get you two settled."

Gaby muttered, "You know everything about the threats, huh?"

Raising her brows, her mother asked, "Do you know me at all, Gabriela?"

Her father came to the rescue at that moment, taking

his wife out from between them and dragging her against his side. He nodded at Ryan. "You must be Ryan. I'm Jorge, Gaby and Jose's father."

"Nice to meet you, sir."

Jorge snorted. "Call me Jorge." He motioned with his head toward the glass sliding door. "Hurry and go grab something to eat out there while you have the chance. My mate and I will join you later."

Her mother began, "Jorge, just wait a minute—"

Jorge cut off his mate. "Give them some time to breathe, Maria. It's going to be hard enough for them to be newly together on PineRock, but add in them staying with us to boot, and it makes it a little trying."

Gaby blinked. "What are you talking about?"

Her father frowned. "Didn't Wes mention that to you? For at least the beginning, you two are staying here with us, along with Jose and Tori. Keeping the humans in one place will make it easier to protect them."

Great. Not only would she have pretty much zero opportunity to be naked with her male inside her parents' house, she'd probably have to deal with Jose's teasing, too. "Do we get any say in this?"

Her father shook his head. "I'm afraid not. I won't risk my children or their mates."

Ryan was at her side, rubbing circles on her lower back. He said, "As much as I hate to admit it, he's right, Gaby. It'll be easier to protect me and your brother's mate this way." He glanced up at her parents. "Although it *is* temporary, right?"

Maria snorted. "Believe me, I'd rather my newly mated children have their own places, too. Walking into a room becomes a dangerous thing until that happens."

Gaby shuddered at the thought. "Ew, Mother, you shouldn't think of such things."

Maria shrugged one shoulder. "It happens to us all. You wouldn't be here otherwise."

Jose sighed. "Come on, Gaby. I think I see Tori out back with Luna. Let's leave before Mom and Dad think of giving some sort of strange dragon and the bees lesson to your human."

From the corner of her eye, she could see Ryan pressing his lips together, trying not to laugh.

The bastard.

Taking his hand, she headed toward the door. "Let's go, Ryan. After you meet Jose's mate, then maybe you can help me tease my brother a little, just because."

"Not unless he wants to irritate someone who can shift into a dragon," Jose stated.

She glanced up. Heaven help her from alpha males.

Her dragon chuckled. *It'll only get worse, as the months roll by and Jose's mate starts to show.*

The only good news is that I'm pregnant now, too. So maybe Jose will be a little nicer to me.

Her dragon snorted. *Good luck with that.*

Her beast curled up into a ball and shut her eyes, leaving Gaby to talk and eat in peace.

Well, as peaceful as a meal with Luna could be. She

loved her cousin, but Luna acted more like her sister and made it her job to irritate the hell out of her.

Exiting the glass sliding door, Gaby made a line straight for Tori and Luna. Her parents were easy. Luna would take a little more fortitude from Ryan.

Not that she doubted her mate. But it had been a long day, and it was only going to get longer.

Ryan's lips would start bleeding soon if he had to keep biting them so he wouldn't laugh.

Gaby had mentioned how her family was close, but hearing about it and seeing it in person were two different things.

Even if he would've preferred not to stay with her parents straight away, he'd instantly liked them. Which was a far cry from his ex-wife's, who had only bothered to meet him once.

The more he thought about it, the more warning signs he'd ignored. But he couldn't get mad any longer. All of those things had brought him to his Gaby, after all.

Gaby waved to a slightly pale woman with dark hair and eyes. She stood next to another woman around Gaby's age who looked a lot like her, except for the shape of the eyes—same dark hair, brown eyes, and light brown skin.

The two women came up to them. When Jose went to the pale woman's side, he figured her to be Tori and the other to be Luna. Tori spoke up. "You're back, Gaby!" She looked at Ryan and smiled. "Hi there."

Jose growled, but the woman lightly elbowed him in the side and murmured, "Behave."

Ryan cleared his throat. "Nice to meet you, ma'am."

The woman snorted. "I'm way too young to be a ma'am. I'm Tori."

The other woman, Luna, slowly studied him from head to toe. "At least you picked a sexy one, Gaby."

"Luna," Gaby growled. "That's *my* male, so don't eye him like a lollipop you want to lick."

Luna smiled at him, her eyes flashing. "Are you super sure you want to be with my cousin? I can promise a little more adventure, in all aspects of our lives, if you get my meaning."

Jose and Gaby both muttered, "Holy crap," but Ryan didn't look away from Luna. "Thanks for the offer, but Gaby is my dragon lady. I'm sure you'll find your own other half at some point."

Gaby's head whipped to him. "You think of me as your other half already?"

Shit, maybe he shouldn't have said that. But he wouldn't take it back. He gazed down at Gaby. "Yes, I do. I know it hasn't been that long, but I can't imagine going back to my lonely house. I'd constantly think of you."

"Ryan," Gaby breathed.

Luna made a gagging sound, ruining the moment. "And this is the guy you want, Gaby? You could've gone for a much bigger rebellion than him."

Gaby glared at her cousin. "We've never had the same taste in males, so why would I want your type? Enter your name next time and maybe you can pick out a bad boy who acts like a bastard until he meets you and turns into a softie for his female. That's your dream, isn't it?"

"I do like a challenge," Luna stated. "Of course, trying to seduce your male away would be the ultimate one."

Gaby growled and looked away from Luna, back at Ryan. "Excuse my cousin's manners. I swear she lives to make my life miserable."

Not caring that any number of people were watching, Ryan raised his free hand to cup Gaby's cheek. "Do you want to find somewhere quiet for a short while, to get away from any stress?" To take a break and let him kiss her as much as he wanted, of course. To add a touch of guilt toward her cousin, he said, "For the baby's sake."

Luna cursed. "That's right, you're pregnant now. I sort of forgot. I'll try to be nicer, but I can't guarantee it. Don't tell my dad how I treated you as he has a big thing for revering pregnant females. Okay?"

Gaby never looked away from his eyes. "Change the playlist to the one I like, and I'll forget everything that just happened."

With a sigh, Luna trudged away.

"What playlist?" he asked.

"That's a long story," Gaby stated. She finally faced

toward her brother and his mate. "Let's sit down together at that table over there to eat, and I'll tell you about it."

"Are you sure you're fine?" He leaned down to whisper. "I wouldn't mind some alone time with you myself."

Jose looked toward the sky. "If you're going to seduce my sister, do it some place where I can't hear you."

Crap, he'd forgotten all about super dragon-shifter hearing.

Tori laughed. "Oh, it wasn't that bad. Now, come on. You have two pregnant women here to feed. I'm sure your dragon doesn't like you starving us and all."

Ryan expected a protest, but Jose merely placed a hand on his mate's back. "Come on. Let's find you something that you can keep down."

Once the pair were a few feet away, Ryan kissed Gaby quickly. "You, too. Even without an inner dragon, my instinct is to keep you and the baby fed."

She raised an eyebrow. "For tonight, I won't argue. Although start acting like my brother, and we may have a few words."

He snorted. "Noted."

As they headed to the barbecued offerings, Ryan smiled at his dragon lady. He'd thought it would be hard to stay with dragon-shifters, away from the humans. And while there was still a lot of challenges to face, so far, he kind of liked it.

He'd miss his sister, but Tiffany was just finishing her master's degree and could move anywhere for an engineering job. He doubted she'd stay in Phoenix.

So Ryan just needed to work as hard as possible to fit in with Gaby's family and to start the seeds of his new life on PineRock. Because no matter if he had to delay the true start of his new life with Gaby—in their own place —for weeks or even months, he wanted it more than anything.

Chapter Eight

The next morning, Gaby woke up in her old childhood bedroom and snuggled against the warm, male chest under her cheek.

While it wasn't quite as good as if it'd been their own place, she would always be happy to wake up next to Ryan.

Her dragon yawned. *He needs to get up, too, so I can shift and show him our dragon form.*

I know you're eager, but he deserves some sleep after the frenzy.

Her beast grunted. *He enjoyed it just as much as we did, so I won't apologize.*

Ryan's voice rumbled inside his chest. "Good morning."

Looking up, she smiled as her male blinked away his sleepiness. "It is with you here."

He grinned and pulled her up so he could kiss her. "I thought I was supposed to be the charming one."

"There's no rule that I can't be charming, too, on occasion."

He placed a possessive hand on her hip. "So what's on the agenda for today? A meeting with the clan leader, but is the rest of it ours?"

She sighed. "I wish. But Cris sent me a text late last night and she wants to meet with us in an hour or so."

He tightened his grip on her. "As long as she's not going to tell me to leave, it should be fine. Although, I was hoping I could see your dragon today."

At the disappointment in his tone, she sat up. "We can still manage that if we hurry. After all, Cris wants to meet at the small landing area near the main security building, so there's plenty of room for me to shift."

He searched her eyes. "Will it be safe there? Ashley mentioned one of the Protectors might be hiding their true intentions."

Gaby tucked a section of hair behind one ear. "It should be. I mean, if they were going to try and harm either of us, they'd wait until we were somewhere more remote and with no witnesses."

He raised his brows. "Why doesn't it surprise me that you've thought of that?"

She placed a hand on his chest and lightly ran her fingers back and forth, loving his now familiar muscles and heat. "Well, what my brother said yesterday, about me not making the best decisions when I was younger, is true. I may, just may, have had a thing for sneaking off PineRock and exploring the outer areas as a teenager.

That's how I saw Clan SkyTree for the first time, albeit from a distance." She sighed. "However, it was also the last time. I got busted on that one, and from there on out, the Protectors and my family watched me super closely, afraid I'd end up in major trouble, or worse."

Ryan placed a hand over hers on his chest and squeezed. "Don't the dragon clans visit with one another? There are a lot around Tahoe—four, I think—and it would help your cousins find their true mates if there was more visiting among them all."

She shrugged one shoulder. "It depends on both what a clan leader and ADDA thinks at any given time. Some of the Tahoe clans fought each other in the not too distant past. Not to mention an early form of ADDA shuffled dragons around willy-nilly, sometimes even taking in outcasts and prisoners from other countries to earn some money, and placed them all over the country."

It was why the US had the most diverse group of dragon-shifters in the world, with Australia being a close second.

Ryan grunted. "Well, once we get everything settled here, maybe we can plant the seed into your mom's head about your cousins finding mates outside the clan and then it'll spread to the rest of the family. With enough people, maybe ADDA and Wes will allow dragons from other clans to visit."

She smiled down at Ryan. "You've been here a day and you're already trying to fix things."

He shrugged. "If my child is going to be a dragon-shifter, then why wouldn't I want to try and start changing things now? Sort of like how some people start saving for college before a kid is even born, except this is a lot more important to my kid's future."

Using her free hand, she traced Ryan's jaw, his cheek, and then his lips. "You are too good to be true, huh?"

He tugged her down and rolled her under him. "No, I'm just an average guy who finally has a future to fight for."

She stopped breathing. At the love and desire in Ryan's eyes, she wished she could do more than kiss him and show how much she wanted him, too.

But as the old porcelain statues and dusty stuffed animals hovered at the edge of her vision, reminding Gaby of where they were, she merely settled for saying, "We'll do it together." She kissed him quickly. "But first, you should see my dragon. If you're going to live with a dragon clan, you need to get over the mix of amazement and fear that comes with us being in our dragon forms. Otherwise, that could be a huge negative for you if a dragon tries to attack you."

After kissing her gently, he murmured, "As if I could ever be afraid of you, Gaby."

Her beast sat up at that. *Maybe just to test his limits, I'll roar and flash some teeth.*

She laughed and Ryan quirked his eyebrows in question. Gaby explained, "You just threw down a challenge to my dragon half. You're going to learn quickly how doing that isn't always the best idea."

He kissed her again. "Then tell your dragon to bring it."

She sighed happily.

Damn, she wanted Ryan all to herself for days, no weeks, and then some. Hell, she'd settle for a few hours.

But since she wasn't about to try and sneak around in her parents' house when everyone should be getting up soon—not all of the walls were soundproofed and her family would hear everything—Gaby motioned to the attached bathroom. "We're going to have to take the fastest showers in history to have enough time for my dragon to try."

He tickled her side and she shrieked. "I can take a shower in a matter of minutes. Maybe I should help you, so it doesn't take forever."

Ryan let her up and Gaby raced to the bathroom.

And even though they were on their best behavior, there may have been some kissing. And definitely some fondling.

They were basically like newlyweds, after all. Although the sooner they could truly be mated and act like it freely in their own house, the better.

RYAN HATED that he had to be vigilant of their surroundings as they walked toward the specified landing area near the security building, but he did it anyway.

There were families walking their children, young

dragons heading toward a three-story building that was probably a school, and quite a few solo dragon-shifters walking to one place or the other, probably on their way to work.

It all seemed so normal. True, every once in a while, a dragon would fly overhead or jump into the air, but dragon-shifters weren't that different from humans. They were all just trying to live their lives to the best of their abilities.

If only more humans would realize that, maybe they'd stop being afraid of them.

Gaby squeezed his hand and he glanced down at his beautiful lady. She pointed to a structure that looked to be a duplex, with two houses sharing a wall. "That's where I live. Or, rather, lived. Now that I have a male and a baby on the way, I'm going to need something with a little more privacy." She lowered her voice to a whisper. "My neighbor is an older dragonwoman who would probably give us looks every morning since the walls are paper thin."

He chuckled. "Yes, let's give the woman her much-needed rest by finding somewhere else to stay once we can leave your parents' place." He studied the front of the duplex, which was painted a light brown with a few shrubs in the front. "Still, I wish we could stop and check it out, though. Just like your room back home, I'm sure it'd give me some insight into who is Gabriela Santos."

She snorted. "Better not, and not just because then I wouldn't have time to show you my dragon. I'm not the

JESSIE DONOVAN

tidiest person in the world, and I was too anxious to get the whole lottery thing started to bother cleaning."

"Later, then. Because I really *do* want to see your dragon, not because a little mess bothers me."

His woman's pupils flashed. Ryan had become well-acquainted with the beast during the frenzy, but only when taking over Gaby's human form.

He wanted to pet and charm her inner beast in her natural element, too. Gaby had mentioned something about scratching behind the ears, so he'd most definitely start there.

He did have a question he'd burned to ask but had held back. No longer. "So I was wondering, will your dragon ever be able to take me up into the air?"

Gaby shrugged. "I honestly don't know. ADDA forbade it once a long time ago and I think it's still against the law."

He pushed aside his disappointment. "Hm, maybe there can be an exception for humans that live with a dragon clan? I know humans still worry about dragon-shifters swooping down to kidnap them, soar up to the sky, and then drop them to their deaths. It's sort of like a bogeyman for anyone who lives near a dragon clan."

Amusement danced in her eyes. "It's hard to imagine I'm the stuff of nightmares."

"So far, no. But I have yet to see your inner dragon dealing with pregnancy hormones."

He winked and she rolled her eyes. "It won't be that

bad. Well, as long as you don't try to piss me off." She sobered. "Did your parents use those stories with you?"

He shook his head. "There aren't any clans close to Dallas where I grew up, so no. But when I moved to Phoenix about fifteen years ago, I heard it mentioned a few times."

Gaby tilted her head. "Well, we'll add it to the ever-growing list of things to persuade ADDA to change. At this rate, it's going to take a few lifetimes to accomplish it all."

He didn't like the defeated-sounding tone of her voice. "Hey, I'm sure we can get your brother's mate to help, and maybe a few others. It won't be just us."

"True. Although, let's keep Luna out of the loop, if we can. She'll probably try to seduce someone from ADDA and then use it to blackmail them to get what she wants."

Because ADDA employees couldn't fraternize with dragon-shifters. Ryan had read that somewhere, not that he could remember where. "I'll keep it from her for now, but I want to get to know Luna myself, too. Sometimes family acts one way with us and a different way with others."

She raised her brows. "But you are family now, Ryan."

"In a way. But I'm also a newcomer, and a human. That might work to my advantage with your cousin."

"Try if you want, but don't get your hopes up," Gaby muttered.

He did his best not to smile.

His dragonwoman motioned ahead of them. "There's the landing area."

The shielded section was probably about the size of two football fields, with low rock walls surrounding it. He noticed little cubby holes in the walls, which explained why it was there—to store their clothes and other belongings. After all, dragons didn't blink twice at nudity, according to Gaby, and they were always naked right before shifting.

Not that he wanted any male to see his woman naked.

Gaby stopped next to a cubby and took off her shoes. He growled. "Do you have to be naked for everyone to see?"

She unbuttoned her jeans. "If we try to shift with clothes on, they rip and get destroyed. And not only is that super wasteful, it would get really, really expensive." He grunted, and she paused to take his hand again. "Don't worry, you're the only one I give a private show to, Ryan. To everyone else here, it's the equivalent of wearing a different outfit. Well, mostly. The teenagers get curious at some point and start paying attention to older dragons for a short while. But from what I've heard, humans do that, too."

True, but he still didn't like it. Maybe he was more like a possessive dragon-shifter than he'd thought. "It'll just take some getting used to, is all. Although it does explain why you don't have any tan lines."

She smiled slowly. "Sometimes, during a break for my job, I shift back to a human and lay in the sun. Another bonus to being a dragon-shifter—we don't get cancer, not even skin cancer."

Thinking of his aunt during his childhood, who'd always plastered everyone with sunscreen to protect against the Texas sunshine, he sighed. "That would be nice."

"Ah, but do you burn or tan? You're not super pale, but pale enough."

"I tan. But between work and my home gym, I didn't spend much time outdoors, even when it wasn't a million degrees outside. Summers in Arizona aren't the best for walking, let alone hiking or running, any place that doesn't have air conditioning."

Leaning over, she kissed his neck and whispered, "Pale or not, you're still the sexiest male alive to me."

Her words, combined with the heat of her lips and her delicious scent of woman and vanilla, blood rushed south.

Thank fuck he didn't have to strip right now in front of everyone.

Gaby glanced down and snorted. "Yeah, that takes some training, too, for the males."

He lightly slapped her ass, and she giggled before shucking the rest of her clothes and stowing them into the cubby.

She walked toward the center, most definitely exaggerating the sway of her hips, and Ryan resisted adjusting himself.

Damn, what he wouldn't give to have their own, private room for a short while. Did dragon-shifters have hotels? He had no idea.

Gaby turned to face toward him and shouted, "Come over anytime after I've shifted, Ryan."

He nodded and waited. A few seconds later, Gaby's body glowed ever so faintly before her nose elongated into a snout, wings sprouted from her back, and her arms and legs morphed into fore and hind limbs. Within a matter of seconds, Gaby stood in her tall dragon form, the sun glinting off her golden scales.

Even though she was big in dragon form—at least to him—she wasn't scary but rather beautiful. The shimmering scales, her slitted pupils, and even the points of her ears were all like a work of art.

She tilted her head in question, and it snapped Ryan out of his trance. He rushed over and tried not to feel too insignificant standing next to her. "You're so beautiful."

She butted her snout against his middle, but obviously not at full force since he barely stepped back at the contact.

Because, after all, she was a freaking dragon who could probably send him crashing into a mountain if she wanted to.

Not that she ever would. He reached up to tentatively touch her snout, loving the smoothness under his fingers. The scales weren't cold to the touch, but not overly warm either. They felt a lot like hard leather. "I bet these get nice and toasty once you've lain in the sun for a while."

She huffed, probably the dragon equivalent of a laugh.

He decided to tease some more, never ceasing the wandering of his hands. "When it gets cold, you could set up a few heat lamps, get some dragons toasty, and then put them in a big room to warm everyone right up."

Gaby's dragon poked him in the back with her tail. "What? There are so many possibilities you haven't thought of. You could probably make a fortune with tourists, if you wanted. 'Feel the inner fire of a dragon today!' Or something like that."

The tail wrapped around his middle and lifted before turning him upside down. Gaby's beast brought him close to one of her big, brown eyes—the same color as when she was human, except the pupils were permanently slitted. The surface reflected both him and the building behind.

Maybe someone would think the large, slitted eye was scary, but he'd seen her dragon enough during the frenzy that it would be strange not to see slitted pupils ever again with his woman. "If you're trying to glare, it's not going to scare me, Gaby."

A female voice behind him said, "Maybe not with her, but with anyone else, it sure as hell should."

Gaby set him down on his feet and he turned, spotting Cris. Before he could ask what she was talking about, the head Protector continued, "And stay in your dragon form, Gaby. Today's all about training your human to defend himself as best as he can with a dragon-shifter in their dragon form."

Ryan frowned. "Is that even possible?"

Cris crossed her arms over her chest. "Yes, and we're going to keep at a few key things until they become second nature."

He glanced at Gaby's golden dragon form. "I'm not going to hurt Gaby, no matter what you say."

Cris grunted. "No one's going to get hurt, but I suppose this means I'm going to need another dragon for you to practice with, then. Should I go bother Wes?"

Gaby bumped his back lightly, and he glanced at her again. She shook her head and tapped her chest.

His woman wanted him to practice with her.

He touched her snout. "Are you sure?" She nodded. "All right, but you better not use it against me later to win an argument."

The dragon did its best shrug and he snorted. Nothing would be off-limits, it seemed.

Still, if he wanted to fight for his future wife and child, he needed to seriously up his game. Defending against a dragon-shifter was just the first step.

He turned back toward Cris. "Okay, I'll do it."

"Good. You won't get everything down in one session, but you'll have lessons with me or Wes every day until we think you're ready. Only when you get the green light from me will you be able to mate Gaby, provided Wes and ADDA can work that out."

Talk about the most important form of motivation. While not a guarantee, it was still the best offer he'd received so far.

Keeping a hand on Gaby's snout, he asked, "So, what's first?"

As Cris put him in position and began his lessons, it didn't take long for Ryan to end up on his ass. Repeatedly.

But as he improved a little each time, his confidence grew. He'd learn this as best he could, for both himself and the woman he loved.

Chapter Nine

Two weeks later, Ryan stood next to Gaby inside PineRock's main landing area. He brushed a few strands of hair off her face. "I wish you didn't have to go back to work. Not because of your job, but because I'll miss you."

She smiled at him. "It did take some convincing for you to accept I won't rush into a fire at the first opportunity, just to prove I'm capable of doing things while pregnant."

He grunted. "I don't have to like something to still support you. Besides, your brother already contacted your bosses to extract a few promises."

She shook her head. "Don't remind me. If you had done it, we may not be talking right now."

He chuckled. "I wouldn't go that far. Although I'd be lying if I didn't say it brought me some peace of mind."

Gaby sighed. "Males—it doesn't matter if you're

human or dragon-shifter, you act the same around your females."

Pulling her against his body, he cupped her cheek and leaned closer to her face. "Just come back to me safe and sound, Gaby. That's all I ask."

She placed a hand on his chest. "I will do everything in my power to. But you have to promise to watch your back. Just because it's been uneventful the last two weeks doesn't mean there still isn't a threat."

They both had figured that if someone wanted to harm Ryan, the perfect time to do it would be when Gaby went back to work.

He gestured toward the two Protectors standing off to the side. "That's why I have them." And the special dragon Taser and emergency call button in his pocket. But he wasn't about to reveal that secret out loud, just in case someone was listening. "But if you don't leave, you'll be late." He kissed her gently. "Call me on your lunch break, if you can."

She bobbed her head. "So I can check up on you."

He smiled. "I think we'll be checking up on each other."

As she grinned at him and made his heart skip a beat, Ryan itched to tell Gaby how he felt. But if he said he loved her now, she'd probably put it down to her returning to work.

However, in the next week he was going to pull out all the stops for a romantic dinner and tell her. Wes had allowed him to stay two weeks so far, but it could change at any moment. And he wasn't going to regret not telling Gaby about his feelings.

She pressed her mouth to his again, and he parted his lips at the feel of her tongue. As soon as she stroked against his, he did the same, the two of them tangling, caressing, possessing one another, as if they couldn't get enough.

Ryan never would, and made sure Gaby could tell from his kiss.

When she finally pulled away, they both breathed heavily. She murmured, "I really do need to leave."

Taking a deep breath, he stepped back. "Then go. The sooner you do, the sooner you'll come home to me."

If Gaby's cousin Luna had been around, she would've made one of those gagging sounds, but Gaby beamed at him, and her reaction was the only one that mattered.

He watched her strip methodically, move to the center of the area, and slowly morph into her golden dragon form. She stared at him for a few beats before crouching down and jumping into the sky.

Even though he'd seen the same maneuver a dozen times by now—all he had to do was ask, and Gaby's dragon loved to come out—it still made his heart skip a beat at her dragon's sheer power and beauty.

When she was finally out of sight, Ryan headed toward his two guards. One of the men was a regular. The guy in his mid-twenties with dark, curly hair and dark skin was named Andre Carter, who was not only

Dr. Carter's younger brother, but he'd also been guarding the Santos's house since day one. However, the pale, brown-haired male with blue eyes was new to Ryan.

Despite the fact there was no reason to suspect anything, Ryan barely resisted reaching for the special Taser gun in his pocket.

He stopped just in front of the two men and said, "As exciting as it is, I just need to get back to the Santos house to do some work myself."

Andre motioned toward the security building. "I need to stop by there first, to change shifts. My sister's about to give birth and Cris gave me permission to go see her."

The way the unfamiliar guy stood a little taller didn't go unnoticed, but for all Ryan knew, this would be the man's first non-grunt work assignment.

Still, his gut said something was off about the guy. His expression was neutral, but every time Ryan moved forward a little, he inched backward, maintaining his distance.

Ryan answered Andre. "Okay, I should check-in with Cris anyway."

Andre motioned with a hand. "Then let's go."

Ryan and his entourage assumed the usual position with him in the center and a Protector in front and behind him, the weight of his Taser in one pocket and the special emergency button in the other.

While he hoped he was only being paranoid, he couldn't be too careful. With Gaby gone, it was time to prove he could live on a dragon clan's land and try to hold his own.

Ryan stood waiting in the reception area of the main security building, doing his best not to tap his foot or show impatience. Cris was a busy person and had more than generously donated her time to train him over the last couple weeks.

And yet, she was one of the few he trusted and he yearned to discuss the new Protector guards with her. He had a bad feeling about the blue-eyed Protector guy—he'd found out his name was Leon—and wanted to ensure he'd been vetted by Cris.

However, when Cris's second-in-command returned with a frown on his face, Ryan knew the dragonwoman wasn't in the building. The Protector stopped next to him and said, "She's not here. Something about a teenager trapped in a cave she had to rescue. I can check to see if Wes is available, if you want."

Wes was even busier than Cris most days.

Thinking of his training and the secret weapons in his pockets, Ryan shook his head. "No, it's all right. But I'll be at the Santos house. Just have Cris call me when she can spare a minute."

"Will do. Feel free to call me if you need me, Ryan."

As the second-in-command walked away, Ryan did his best to school his face into a neutral expression. The walk wouldn't take more than ten or fifteen minutes. As long as he could survive that, then he could work on his latest code and forget about danger for a while. Two of Gaby's uncles should be at the house, along with a few of their children. They'd act as a buffer, and if it came to it, the uncles would protect him.

Ryan approached Leon, who was standing with another new face he'd never met before—a male with black hair, golden beige skin, and brown eyes. They stopped talking as soon as he reached them.

For all he knew, they could've just been discussing regular dragon-shifter duties. Ryan couldn't let his imagination get the better of him.

Be smart and it'll be fine. Ryan smiled and motioned ahead. "Come on, let's get a move on. The sooner I get home, the sooner you two can watch videos on your phone or do whatever it is you do while standing outside the house."

Neither elaborated or even smiled. Okay, so there'd be no charming or building rapport with the two dragon-shifters.

As they walked the usual route toward Gaby's parents' house, Ryan remained on edge. Something was going to happen, he was sure of it. But without any sort of proof, no one would believe him. Hell, accusing two Protectors could make the few dragons he'd won over turn against him.

So he just kept walking. However, some of his fears were confirmed when a giant pile of firewood, enough to probably keep a house warm for an entire winter, blocked the path going through the center of PineRock's land.

Leon grunted. "We'll go the long way."

Ryan gestured toward the pile. "We can just climb over it. The rock walls to either side aren't that tall."

Leon shook his head once. "No, I can't risk you breaking your neck. A few extra minutes walking won't kill you."

Ryan eyed the ginormous wood pile. "Then let's clear it. I could do with some exercise."

"You're supposed to be home, and that's where you're going. Now, come on," Leon stated.

Given the warnings Ryan had received over the last couple weeks, the whole situation was suspicious, for sure. And Ryan was tempted to climb the wall anyway.

However, Leon grabbed his upper arm and tugged. "This way. If I'm forced to babysit some human, then I'll do it. But it also means you're going to listen to me."

Okay, that statement kicked up his unease. Between Cris's absence, the suspicious roadblock and the new guards manhandling him, something was definitely up.

He couldn't outrun a dragon-shifter, though. And given their training with the US Army before becoming Protectors, they probably could incapacitate him before he could shout a word.

Ryan's best option was to go along with the pair and try to take them by surprise.

Sure, he'd have to be quick to use the Taser on one

and then the other, or tase one and then press the emergency transmitter before the other attacked, but they were the only options available to handle the situation.

So Ryan let the Protector guide him down a different path, one that wound through some trees situated at the edge of the clan.

Trees he'd rather liked before as he'd escaped with Gaby a few times to them. But now he saw them for the threat they were—under their cover, the two dragons could do anything to him, with no one the wiser.

And if his gut was right about them, Ryan had no chance once they reached the tree cover.

When Leon tugged him harder and dug in what had to be talons into his bicep, not caring if he drew blood, Ryan decided to play it safe even if he didn't have any proof beyond his gut. Their behavior wasn't normal for Protectors he'd met before. Not to mention how Cris had ordered for Ryan not to be harmed under any circumstances.

He had to act soon, while he still had the chance.

Taking a deep breath, Ryan tried to focus as Cris had taught him. Ignoring his pounding heart wasn't easy, but the image of Gaby smiling at him helped.

Because he'd never see that image again if he died.

Eventually the Protector released Ryan's arm, which throbbed like hell at this point from the talon marks, but only to stay at his side. The other Protector, who had been walking behind him, moved to his other side.

If Ryan was going to make a move, it was now or never.

He casually put his hands inside his pockets. Leon reached for him, but Ryan managed to press the emergency button with one hand and took out the Taser with another. He ducked, rolled to the side, and then jumped for the nearest dragon-shifter—Leon—his Taser at the ready.

Once he tumbled to the ground with the dragon-shifter, he pressed the device against his opponent's skin, dug in the special barbs to keep it in place, tried his best to untangle himself, and pressed the button.

He had two seconds to move, and he rolled away just as electricity raced through the dragon-shifter and he stopped moving.

Ryan looked for the other one but couldn't see him.

Grateful for the adrenaline, he jumped to his feet and ran the opposite way. He'd nearly gotten back to the main path when a green dragon appeared in the sky. In a split second, the beast had swooped down, scooped Ryan up in his talons, and flapped its wings to head skyward.

As the ground grew smaller and smaller, fear crept over him.

All the dragon had to do was drop him and he was dead.

And sure enough, about sixty seconds later, the dragon did exactly that and Ryan screamed as he raced toward the ground.

Another dragon swooped down and plucked him

from the air, the force of the talons against his chest sending excruciating pain through his body and he heard a crack.

Before he could do more than notice that the dragon was slowly descending toward the landing area, Ryan blacked out.

Chapter Ten

Gaby paced the length of the small, private waiting room inside the clinic and dug her nails into her palms in impatience. Ryan had been in surgery for five hours already, and she'd yet to receive an update.

Her dragon said softly, *Dr. Carter will tell us when there's news. It's better for him to focus solely on Ryan right now.*

Even though she knew that was true, Gaby growled, *A nurse could tell us something, anything, about his condition. Even if it's only how there's no change, that would be something.*

Wisely, her dragon said nothing.

They'd argued back and forth the entire return flight to PineRock, about how her dragon hadn't wanted to leave Ryan alone and Gaby assuring her beast that he'd be fine with all the protections in place.

In the end, Gaby had been dead wrong. Although it did help her feel a little better that even Cris had been fooled by the traitors.

The human haters had gone to the extent of snapping the bones of one of their children and putting the boy inside a cave for Cris to rescue.

Not even the fact the traitors were all being held, awaiting ADDA to collect them, helped ease her anger and fear.

Because it was entirely possible that Ryan would end up either paralyzed, or could even die. Snatching a human body from free fall wasn't easy to begin with, and probably few, apart from Cris, could have managed it without killing him.

Gaby was still beyond grateful that Cris had been on her way home when she'd spotted one of her Protectors carrying Ryan into the air.

She shuddered to think what would've happened if Cris had approached PineRock a few minutes later.

Her dragon spoke up again. *Stop wondering about what could've been. Ryan is still alive, and that's all that matters.*

For now. *I don't know how you can be so calm.*

I have faith in our human. Besides, there is a major upside from it all—Wes has discovered the last of the traitors within the clan.

I wish I could be happy about that. But I just want Ryan to wake up again.

It'd been hard enough leaving him to go back to work, but to only be called back soon after and told he might die had made Gaby realize something important.

She loved Ryan Ford. And now, she might never get the chance to tell him.

Tears prickled her eyes, but in the next instant, her

mother returned from the cafeteria. She must've noticed Gaby's tears even from across the room and rushed to her side. "Oh Gaby, come here."

Needing her mother's touch, she hugged her close and let some of her tears fall. As her mom stroked her hair, she murmured, "Your human is strong. I have faith he'll pull through."

"But he might not."

"Now, Gabriela Santos, what have I said all these years about not giving up on the things you love?"

She sniffled. "We cherish them and fight to our last breath to protect them."

Her mom leaned back to meet her gaze again. "That's right. So do as I taught you. Be strong and fight the best way you can—by believing in him and Dr. Carter. And once Ryan opens his eyes, you let him know he's not going anywhere, either, so he'd better not think of dying for many, many decades to come. And even that will be negotiable."

Gaby nearly argued that positive thinking wasn't enough sometimes, but held back. Her mother was only trying to help. And the fact her mom so wholeheartedly endorsed Ryan meant a lot to her.

She nodded. "Oh, believe me, when he wakes up, I'm not letting him out of my sight any time soon."

Her mother raised her brows. "For a short while, yes. But don't let the traitors win in the long run. If you fear living your life going forward, they will have won, no matter if they're locked up somewhere or not."

Gaby frowned. "That's easy for you to say—Dad is a dragon-shifter and can more easily overcome threats from within the clan. However, Ryan can't change his form and it's simply a fact that he's weaker. I can't just disregard that bit and pretend everything will work out."

Her mother raised her brows. "Your human did a pretty good job after such a short period of training. I'm sure Cris and Wes will arm him further, and train him harder, once this is done. Even if Wes is pretty sure he's cleaned out the last of the clan who want to harm your mate and Jose's—thanks to confessions—he's not going to take any chances."

She opened her mouth to argue, but Dr. Carter entered the room still wearing his scrubs. Both she and her mother turned toward him and he spoke before they could ask anything. "Ryan is alive. I repaired the internal damage and he should heal fully from that, but a few spinal fractures showed up on the X-ray. I won't know for sure the extent of the damage until he's awake and we can test if he's paralyzed from the waist down, or at all."

Her mother gripped her hand and Gaby squeezed back, taking comfort. Gaby blurted, "When can I see him?"

Dr. Carter replied, "He won't be awake for a while, but if you want to sit next to his bed and hold his hand, you can follow me now. However, you have to promise not to jostle him or do more than hold his hand or maybe gently touch his face at this point. Since he's human, the fractures will take a lot longer to heal even with dragon's blood injections and I don't want to risk any more damage."

With a dragon-shifter, they'd probably be up and about within a few days after a similar injury.

It was yet another disadvantage her human possessed.

At least dragon's blood sped up the healing process in humans a little. Gaby would give as much as she needed to get him healthy ASAP. "I promise to follow any order you have, but just let me see my male."

Dr. Carter motioned with a hand. "Then follow me."

Gaby barely paid attention as she followed the head doctor down the corridor. She somehow went through the motions of washing her hands, too, before finally reaching the room. Dr. Carter said quietly, "Just remember he looks worse than he is, Gaby. The bruises will heal within a day or two thanks to the injection of dragon's blood you gave us."

The doctor's words made her heart pound harder. She had been able to at least do that. Gaby bobbed her head. "Just let me see him."

He finally allowed Gaby into the room and she drew in a breath.

Ryan was paler than normal, his face and arms a mottle of bruises, not to mention a bandage around one of his upper arms poking from under his hospital gown. A brace was around his neck, and he had various machines hooked up to him.

It took everything Gaby had not to start crying again. She needed to be strong for her male.

Dr. Carter whispered, "He's breathing on his own, which is good. The rest of the machines are just keeping track of his vitals." He gently pushed her toward the bed. "Go. Your mate will sense you're near and it'll help him."

Swallowing, Gaby moved to the bedside and gently took Ryan's hand. It was cooler than she liked, but the steady rise and fall of his chest helped ease the worst of her fears.

Her dragon spoke up. *Talk to him. Corny as it sounds, our voice could help his healing process. Let him know we're here and won't walk away from him.*

Why would you even suggest we'd leave him?

Because some people wouldn't be able to handle this so soon after meeting.

Ryan is our mate, even if we haven't had our official ceremony yet. I won't abandon him because of a few injuries.

Her dragon grunted in approval and fell silent.

Once the doctor left her, Gaby gently touched his cheek and said, "I'm here, Ryan. You were brave to try and fight them, and I couldn't be prouder. But do you know what will make me even prouder to be your mate? If you wake up and heal as quickly as possible. Wes has most of the threats under control and we might even be able to finally have our own place. That should be a strong enough motivation for you, I think, to not have to try and sneak around in my parents' house."

Silence, except for the whirring of the machines and Ryan's breathing.

Tears rolled down her cheeks, but Gaby quickly wiped them away. She'd done enough crying over the last few hours. Ryan needed her to be strong, and she would be.

So she sat down and kept talking, telling him stories about her, her family, and even some of the dragon-shifter legends she'd learned as a child.

While she had no proof that it helped, she believed that it did. She'd do a hell of a lot more to get her male to wake up again.

RYAN HEARD some sort of muffled sound, and it brought him out of a deep sleep.

His eyelids were heavy, though, and he merely laid there as the sound became clearer and clearer, until he recognized Gaby's voice.

"And that's how dragon-shifters came to be in North America. It seems a little far-fetched to me, but it sure makes for a good story."

Gaby. The attack and his fall came rushing back. He was alive, and his woman was right next to him.

Ryan tried his best to open his eyes. After a few beats, he finally managed to do it. Gaby's beautiful eyes came into view and she gasped. "Ryan! You're awake."

He tried to make his mouth work, but his tongue was heavy and mouth dry. All he managed was a croak.

Gaby released his hand and crossed to a small freezer, returning with a cup of something. As she took an ice chip from the cup, she put it at his lips. "The doctor said to give you a few of these when you woke up. It should make it easier to talk."

He gratefully took the cool piece, and once the ice melted and he swallowed, he tried talking again. This time he managed to say, "Gaby, I love you."

She frowned. "Don't go saying your goodbyes, Ryan Ford. I love you, too, but you're going to tell me later, on a real date, when you're not hooked up to machines and wearing a gown that has your ass hanging out."

Probably thanks to some sort of drugs, he smiled without too much pain. "You could turn it around, if you like, and have your way with me."

She snorted. "You're such a male. Here you are, lying in bed with a broken back, and you want to have sex. Sorry, but as sexy as you are in a neck brace—ha ha—you're going to have to wait."

Ryan tried to laugh, but it turned into a groan. "I feel as if I've been hit by a semitruck. So don't make me laugh."

She touched his cheek and leaned over to gently kiss his lips before sitting back beside his bed. "I'll try, but it's better than me ranting about what happened, isn't it? I don't want to make your blood pressure go up."

Her hand found his and Ryan managed to squeeze her fingers. It didn't escape him that it took a hell of a lot of effort to do so, but at least he wasn't completely paralyzed. "Tell me what happened, love. I remember most of it, but it all turns blank as soon as I was snatched from midair."

Gaby sighed. "You have Cris to thank for that."

As Gaby went on to explain about the traitors, their using a child to make their ruse believable, and Cris and Wes cleaning up the remaining bastards within hours, Ryan did his best to stay calm. He wanted to be angry—hell, he wanted to shout—but he wasn't in the best health and he needed to get better to have that real date with Gaby and tell her his feelings again.

When she finally finished, Gaby added, "So now it's just the matter of getting you better."

He forced himself to ask, "And once I do, will I be able to stay?"

Gaby bobbed her head. "Wes thinks so. He's talking with Ashley Swift today, to see if he can come to an agreement with ADDA. It'll be tricky, given how you almost died and all at the hands of a dragon-shifter, but Wes is going to try his best to make it happen. He feels he owes you that, and a lot more, to make up for what happened."

He squeezed Gaby's fingers again. "If he can get me to stay, that's enough. I don't think either Wes or Cris could've predicted someone hurting a child to get to me."

Gaby narrowed her eyes and growled. "No, and thankfully none of them will have children to hurt anymore. ADDA will lock them away for a really long time, or possibly send them to that tiny, isolated island in the Pacific Ocean, the one used for the worst dragon offenders in the world."

He was about to ask more about the dragon-shifter prison island he'd never heard of when Dr. Carter walked into the room and said, "You're awake, Ryan. That's a good sign and shows us the dragon's blood is doing its magic."

"Dragon's blood?" Ryan echoed.

He raised his brows. "Gaby didn't tell you yet? She gave you some, to help you heal. I'm not sure how much it'll help with your back, but it will certainly speed up the rest of your healing."

Gaby turned toward the doctor. "He can squeeze my hand, so that's a good sign, right?"

"It's proof he's not completely paralyzed, but I'm going to need to do a few tests to say anything further." Dr. Carter moved his gaze to Ryan's. "I know you must be exhausted, but do you have enough energy to try a few things for me?"

"If it can tell me whether I can walk again or not, then I'd endure a hell of a lot worse."

"Good." He walked to the base of Ryan's bed. "Gaby, while I won't ask you to leave, move to the side for a few minutes. I need Ryan's full attention for my tests."

After she kissed his cheek, Gaby let go of his hand. Selfish as it was, Ryan wanted to snatch it back.

However, he focused on Dr. Carter and awaited the

tests. Finding out if he was paralyzed or not was more important right then and there.

"Okay, close your eyes and tell me if you feel anything, and where."

Ryan complied, his heart speeding up a fraction, hoping he could feel something.

Then a sharp point stuck into his calf. "Ow."

"Where was it?"

"My calf."

"Good. Now, wait for another jab."

Never in his life had Ryan wanted to feel someone stab him.

One beat passed, and then another. Finally he felt something at the bottom of his foot. "Something on my foot, although it didn't feel sharp."

"Good again. It was the end of my pencil. Open your eyes." Once he complied, the doctor continued, "The early tests are promising, but I can't guarantee you won't have trouble walking or other tasks until you heal enough to try them."

He tried not to let hope overwhelm him as he asked, "When will that be?"

"We'll take it day by day. And yes, I know that's not the answer you want to hear. But if you think yelling or threatening will make me give you a different answer, let alone you trying to hide your health to appear well before you actually are, then you'll be sorely disappointed. I've had to deal with Wes and Cris's injuries before, and didn't give in. You don't stand a chance, human."

The words were said with humor, not threats. Ryan sighed. "Fine. But I'm going to keep asking when we can do the next step every chance I get. I don't like waiting and doing nothing."

Dr. Carter snorted. "Welcome to the club." He looked at Gaby. "You can stay at his side. One of the nurses will bring some food a little later for you both. I'll leave it to you to ensure he eats it."

"Of course, Dr. Carter." Gaby moved back to Ryan's side and took his hand again. The heat of her skin helped him relax. "Give me any task and I'll make sure it gets done."

With a laugh, the doctor left the room.

Gaby stared down at him, and he could tell there were tears in her eyes. "Shh, darling. Everything's going to be okay."

She sniffed. "We're both fighters, so of course we'll do our best. But there's still the chance you won't fully recover. And in a way, it's my fault."

"Don't say that, Gaby. You can't watch me every second of every day, no more than I can you. You merely standing by my side now, regardless of the eventual outcome, is all that matters to me."

It was on the tip of his tongue to say he loved her again, but he decided to keep the feelings until he could take her on a date.

Which meant doing everything he could to get better. Even if he ended up needing a wheelchair for the rest of his life, he'd find a way to make it work.

Just like his sister had never given up on him, he'd never give up on Gaby or their child. They were his family now.

His dragon lady tilted her head. "Of course I'm going to be by your side. You're my human, Ryan, mine." Gaby leaned down to kiss him before standing up straight again. He smiled at his woman, and when she did the same, it raised his spirits a fraction.

Gaby cleared her throat before she spoke again. "With that settled, then there's just one more thing. Once you're a little better, I'll need to call your sister."

He could just imagine her hovering on the other side of his bed. "No, don't worry Tiffany. She has to finish her dissertation before summer or she won't graduate. Letting her know about my condition will only distract her."

She raised an eyebrow. "So you want to keep your injuries a secret from your sister? The one, I might add, who is the whole reason you entered the lottery and brought us together?"

He sighed. "I'm injured. Aren't you supposed to save the guilt trip for later?"

Gaby grinned. "Nope."

He started to laugh, but the pain in his middle made him stop. Stupid injuries. "At least give me a few days so I at least look less like a mottled monster."

His dragon lady gently brushed hair back from his face. "I don't see a monster. Nope, just the sexiest male I know. True, you have a few temporary marks here and there, but it'll take more than that to fool me and my dragon."

And just like that, he said screw keeping his feelings to himself until he was better. "I love you so much, Gabriela Santos. Don't ever change."

She smiled. "I won't, but we're still having that date, even if Cris and Wes have to stand guard ten feet away, to ensure we're protected, we're doing it."

What he wouldn't give to lift her hand to his mouth and kiss it. "We can have as many dates as you like. But I'll let you know now that at the end of the first one, I'm a sure thing. So there's no need to wear any underwear."

She snorted. "Good to know. Make sure you do the same."

As visions of him tossing up her skirt and claiming her while they were both mostly still clothed rushed through his mind, his cock started to stir. "Don't tempt me so early."

Leaning down, she kissed him. "Let's call it an incentive for you to get better faster."

"Maybe some more dragon's blood will help? Your flashing eyes tell me you're eager for me to get the all-clear, too."

She laughed. "We'll see, my human. We'll see."

As he tried to memorize every inch of his woman's face, his eyes started to droop. He didn't want to go back to sleep, but his body was reaching its limit.

Gaby kissed him again and murmured, "Sleep, Ryan. I'll be here to watch over you. And then you can dream about whether I'll still be wearing panties or not when you wake up."

He tried to groan, but it died quickly when pain shot through his body. "Tease."

"And you love it. Now, sleep."

Even though rationally he knew Gaby didn't possess any special magic to make him follow orders, his eyelids slid closed. The last thing he heard was her humming an unfamiliar tune before he passed out.

Chapter Eleven

Wes Dalton leaned against his desk and crossed his arms over his chest, readying himself for what he needed to do, no matter how much he didn't want to do it.

He was about to ask Ashley Swift for another fucking favor.

His dragon grunted. *Don't be so surly. She grows closer to PineRock and our people with each visit. She'll help us out.*

I hope you know that just because she likes the clan doesn't mean she'll ever be ours.

Wes and his dragon had known for over three years that Ashley was their true mate. However, she'd have to give up her position in ADDA and everything she'd ever worked toward to be his mate.

Not to mention Wes would face backlash from ADDA not only for himself, but possibly his clan as well. Which he could never risk.

It was a no-win situation.

His inner beast huffed. *I know you won't try to claim her, even though I don't understand why you hold back—surely two smart people could put their heads together and figure out a solution.*

There isn't one.

I would say you're wrong, but you won't listen to me on this. However, I won't stop looking at her or commenting on how much I want her. It's not my fault if you give up too easily.

He resisted growling at the insult, knowing his dragon did it on purpose.

Even a year ago, Wes would've tried to convince his inner dragon to forget about Ashley. Sometimes a dragon-shifter could move on and the true mate pull would fade with time.

However, three years apart had done nothing. The first time he'd seen her again a couple months ago, the pounding need to kiss and fuck her had reappeared, just like with their original meeting. And it'd taken every iota of strength he'd possessed not to pull her close and claim her.

Wes was fairly sure the pull would never fade for him. Which meant he'd never get his own mate-claim frenzy or to enjoy the female fate had thought his best chance at happiness.

Stop it, he reminded himself. He had a lot of work left to do for PineRock. The needs of over a thousand people were more important than his own.

His beast harrumphed at that thought, no doubt

thinking it merely an excuse. Wes was about to warn his beast to be quiet when the female in question strode through the door.

Ashley wore her usual black trouser pants and button-up shirt, this time a dark blue. He tried his best not to glance to her round hips, or to lust after the breasts he ached to palm. But in the end, he couldn't resist a peek.

She was so fucking perfect. No other female would ever compare to her.

And his dragon promptly sent an image of them sucking one of her hard nipples into their mouth, and Wes said, *Do that again and I'll put you in a mental prison.*

Fine. But it's all your own fault, not mine.

His beast settled down just as her voice filled the room and he focused solely on her face. "You summoned?" she drawled.

The fact she didn't comment on his eyes only bespoke how accustomed she was to being around dragon-shifters. One of the first rules of politeness was to not ask about what an inner dragon said, unless you knew the person well enough. He gestured to the chair in front of him. "Yes, I did. So take a seat."

She crossed her arms and remained standing. "I don't have a lot of time right now, Wes, what with ADDA coming to collect their new prisoners. What do you want?"

"I need another favor." She raised her dark brows,

but he pushed on before she could say anything. "Given what happened to Ryan, I'm not sure if ADDA will let him stay. But I need you to find a way to make it happen so he can mate Gaby."

She searched his gaze a second before answering, "That's going to require me calling in a lot of favors. Which means I'm upping my request from the last time you asked me to work my magic."

He resisted a sigh. "I already said one of the males will participate in the charity auction for orphans, and spend the evening with whomever bids the most. What else do you want now?"

She bobbed her head. "Yes, you gave me that. But now, if I do this, I want you to be the volunteer up for auction."

He blinked. "Me? You're joking, right?"

She shrugged one shoulder. "Why would I? Just think how much more money would come in for not just a night out with a dragonman, but a clan leader. And since the cause is to help orphaned dragon-shifter children, I don't see why you'd say no."

His dragon spoke up. *She seems eager for you to say yes. Maybe she wants to bid on us.*

Dream on, dragon. Wes focused back on Ashley. "Will ADDA even allow it?"

"It's not against the rules. It's also only for one evening, one which won't take place for quite a few months down the line. Your clan should be secure enough for you to leave for a few hours by then, especially if I'm helping you."

Some might think her arrogant, but Wes had seen Ashley work a miracle or two over the years with ADDA. She had more connections than anyone else he knew or ever met.

His dragon chimed in again. *Not only will it help the charity raise funds, we could spend a night in Reno. I can't remember the last time you left PineRock.*

Wes remembered—it'd been almost four years ago, before he'd become clan leader.

And if he were honest with himself, he missed the occasional trip to the busy city, full of lights and noise he'd never hear here in the isolated wilderness. Not to mention watching the humans in the city was always amusing to him since they were similar to dragon-shifters in many ways, but different in others.

Wes made his decision and grunted. "Provided Pine-Rock is safe and I can establish adequate security, I'll do it. But if another major incident or emergency crops up, then you'll let me send one of my other clan members in my stead."

Ashley smiled and put out a hand. "I'll take that deal."

Wes wanted to avoid touching her skin since it'd stir up his dragon, but he couldn't afford to upset the human right now. So he reached out and took her hand. The instant her warm, soft skin touched his, electricity raced up his arm and down to between his legs.

He could also hear Ashley's heart rate skip up at the same time her pupils dilated a fraction.

Fuck, she felt the connection, too, which made resisting her all the harder.

Before his dragon could suggest something ridiculous, like kissing her, he let go and retreated to behind his desk. "Thank you. If there's anything else I can do, let me know."

She searched his gaze a second before replying, "I'll keep that in mind."

With that, Ashley turned and walked out of his office.

Once the door clicked closed, he leaned back in his chair and sighed. While he was grateful that Gaby might get to keep her human for good, Wes wasn't looking forward to the auction.

Because a small part of him wanted Ashley to be there bidding on him. And he knew that could only spell disaster. If he had one night with her, he might never be able to walk away again. And not just because of the frenzy, either.

He'd wanted her sassy smile and quips every day for the rest of his life.

Wes would just have to hope Ashley didn't show up at the event. After all, she worked with dragon-shifters almost every day. Why would she want to spend a night out with one?

His dragon huffed. *Taking care of humans and dragons is one thing, but spending a night out and having fun with a dragon-shifter is a different thing entirely.*

It doesn't matter. I'm the last person she'd want to spend money on just to be in my company.

If you say so.

Done arguing with his beast, Wes sat up and focused on his never-ending mountain of paperwork. His clan was all that mattered. He needed to remember that.

Chapter Twelve

G aby was tempted to take out the note in her pocket again, to double-check that Ryan had asked her to meet him at the lakeside glass observation building. But she'd read it fifty times already and knew this was the right time and place.

And even though her human had survived wearing a back brace for six weeks and another three grueling weeks of physical therapy, she was anxious. He could trip and get hurt again. Or, maybe someone would accidentally bump him and hurt him that way.

Her inner dragon growled. *Just stop it. Dr. Carter cleared him. And thanks to regular shots of our blood, he healed much faster than a regular human. He's as good as new.*

I want to believe that, but…

Keep hovering, and it'll drive him crazy. You can only use your pregnancy hormones as an excuse so many times.

Gaby instinctively placed her hand over the tiniest

bump of her belly. She was about three months pregnant, and in perfect health.

Well, apart from morning sickness and the ups and downs of her emotions. It was bad enough that she'd been regulated to desk work for her job, at the order of her human boss, without a dragon-shifter interfering at all.

She hated desk work. But Gaby knew she could put people's lives in danger with any decision she made out in the field. Besides, she'd be back after the baby was born.

Before she could count how many long months that was, she saw Ryan walking toward her, no cane in sight. She smiled and rushed over to him but stopped short of jumping into his arms.

Ryan raised his brows, patted his chest, and she leaned against him. He kissed her head and murmured, "I won't break, Gaby."

"Logically I know that. But it's still instinctive to be gentle with you."

He moved his lips to her ear, his hot breath against her skin. "Later tonight, I'm going to prove to you I want more than gentle."

Her breath hitched. While they'd been creative over the last three months, Ryan hadn't been cleared for sex until earlier this morning.

And Gaby desperately wanted to strip him right then and there to claim her male.

However, Ryan had asked for that real date she'd wanted and she'd somehow survive it before jumping him. After all, they were having dinner inside a glass structure, for crying out loud. She wasn't about to give the clan a free show.

Her dragon turned smug. *It wouldn't bother me.*

Don't even try to convince me of doing it.

Then hurry up with dinner, or I may just try to take control.

Ryan leaned back and smiled down at her. "I would ask about your flashing eyes, but I have a feeling I know what your dragon wants. So just let her know that she'll get it soon enough."

Her beast hummed. *There's a reason I like him.*

Gaby raised her brows. "Great. With that comment, you're all but asking her to take control."

He kissed her gently. "Not yet, but maybe later."

Yes, her dragon hissed.

Ryan turned so that she was at his side. "Come on or our dinner will get cold."

They started walking the short distance to the glass building. "We could've had a romantic dinner at home, you know."

"No way. After standing by my side for the past excruciating few months, you deserve something more than dinner at home."

She laid her head on his shoulder. "I have you, and that's enough."

He hugged her tighter against her side. "I don't think I can tell you enough how much I love you, Gaby. And since we're finally on that real date, maybe you'll believe me? I'm far from dying, after all."

She lightly slapped his side. "I've believed you since the first time you said it, but I just needed to give you a reason to fight."

He placed his free hand over her lower abdomen. "I would've done anything for you and the baby. Never think I need more than you two."

"Ryan," she breathed.

"It's true. Gaby, you're my whole world. And if me surviving a dragon dropping me from the sky and a broken back isn't enough to convince you, then I'll just have to think of how else I can prove it to you."

Gaby stopped and turned to face her male. "You don't need to try and convince me. I love you, Ryan Ford. Just try not to get yourself killed anytime soon. That's all I need."

The corner of his mouth ticked up. "I'll do my best."

"See that you do." She lifted her face to kiss him, but she pulled away before he could deepen it. "I can smell the pasta and garlic bread from here, and little junior approves. So let's hurry up and eat."

He brushed her hair over her shoulder. "I hope so because vomiting isn't really my type of foreplay, darling."

She punched his arm this time. "Don't even mention it, or you'll jinx it."

"Okay, okay. We're going to have a perfect dinner."

He held open the door to the glass building, and she remembered their first day together, when he'd pulled out the chair for her, and smiled. "At least now I know it's manners and not you trying to pull some sort of power play on me."

Ryan snorted. "That was an interesting first meeting, for sure." Once they were inside, he added, "Add in me free-falling through the sky, and we have quite the story to tell our kid, don't we?"

She smiled. "Yes, but let's hope it doesn't get any more complicated."

Ryan must have reserved the large room for them since no one else was there, just a table with some candles and dishes. With the sun setting, highlighting the peaks surrounding the clan, and the glow from the candles, it was the most romantic thing she'd ever seen.

He pulled out the chair and as she slid into it, she said, "Did you plan this yourself or did you get a little help?"

He grinned. "I did it myself."

Then he went down on one knee—a huge feat he wouldn't have been able to do even three weeks ago—and Gaby's heart skipped a beat. Ryan then took out a small wooden box, the type used to hold dragon mating rings, and opened it. Inside were two silver bands, engraved with words in the old dragon language.

Blinking back tears, she murmured, "Ryan."

"Gaby, you are the bravest, smartest, most beautiful woman I've ever met. While I'll admit I was a bit skeptical at first that anything could work between us, it just clicked. And even when faced with me possibly being paralyzed, you stood by my side. I couldn't ask for a more loyal or loving person to be my wife or mate. So I ask you —will you accept my mate claim?"

"Of course I will, but there aren't any witnesses. So it won't be official."

He held up the ring meant for her. "I can do this again later, the proper way. But for now, will you answer my question?"

She put out her hand, her fingers spread. "Of course I will."

He slid the cool metal over her finger and kissed the band. When he looked up and met her gaze, love burning in his eyes, tears threatened to fall.

Not yet, little one. Let me get through this.

Taking a deep breath, she plucked the other ring from the box and said, "While I had looked forward to the lottery for years, I never imagined it'd bring me the love of my life. You're brave, loving, sweet, and even funny on occasion. Add in how you seem to understand me in a way no one else does, and I've hit the jackpot with my true mate. I love you, Ryan Ford, with every-thing I have. Will you accept my mate claim?"

Smiling, he put his hand up, spread his fingers, and gave an exaggerated wave of them. She snorted, loving how he could make her laugh even during their fake ceremony, and slid the ring on his finger.

She interwove her fingers with his and leaned forward, until her lips were an inch away from his. "Even if it's not quite legally binding yet, you will always be the mate of my heart. So kiss me already."

His lips quirked before he closed the distance between them and kissed her.

She opened immediately, loving how her male stroked against her tongue, letting her know how much he wanted her. Even though they'd probably kissed thousands of times by now, Ryan had a way of making it feel like it was the first each and every time.

She sighed and he took the kiss deeper as he cupped the side of her face.

Just as she was about to move to the floor, he broke it, their breaths mingling for a second before shades descended on the windows.

Gaby blinked. "When were those put in?"

Ryan raised a small remote in his free hand. "In the last couple weeks. I'm sure we're not the only ones who'll take advantage of the privacy."

She bit her lip to keep from laughing. "Everyone will know what's going on now."

He shrugged. "It doesn't bother me if it doesn't you."

She kneeled in front of him before looping her hands behind his neck. "No. So kiss me and claim me in all ways, Ryan. I'm more than ready."

He growled. "You don't have to ask me twice."

With that, he kissed her and slowly lowered her to the ground. And as he both claimed her and then let her dragon do the same with him, Gaby forgot all about the food or anything else but the man she loved with her whole heart above her.

Epilogue

Six Months Later

RYAN STARED down at his newborn son, barely noticing the laughter, teasing, and even soft music playing inside Gaby's hospital room.

He and his mate had barely had time to name their son Mateo Owen before her family had argued their way inside and set up camp.

Not that he minded, but as he touched his son's soft cheek again, he barely heard Gaby's mother say, "It's my turn to hold my grandson."

Ryan shook his head. "Not yet."

He could feel his mother-in-law staring, but for once, he didn't care.

For years he'd wanted a child and had eventually thought he'd never have one.

Then Gaby had walked into his life and given him not only her love, but now a perfect little boy with dark hair. He rather hoped he ended up with Gaby's brown eyes, too, although she had all but ordered her womb to produce a child with hazel eyes like him.

Bringing his son closer, he kissed his forehead.

Gaby touched his arm and he forced his gaze to his mate. Although there were smudges under her eyes from exhaustion, she smiled up at him. "I know you wanted a daughter, but I think you might be taken with Mateo despite him being a boy."

He sat on the edge of Gaby's bed, readjusted his son to fit in the crook of one arm, and placed his free hand on Gaby's cheek. "I'll love any child that's part you, Gabriela Santos-Ford."

She placed her hand over his. "I know. And maybe next time, we'll finally get a girl to help even the odds a little in my family. There are entirely too many males."

His heart warmed as he searched her eyes. "Even after just delivering this little fella, you want to do it all over again?"

She nodded. "Family is important to both of us. I'd rather like to have a big one, if you're up for it."

He kissed her gently. "I am." He brought Mateo down so they could stare at him together. "But let's spoil him a little first."

They barely had a few seconds to stare adoringly at

their son before a familiar woman's voice cut through the room. "Ryan!"

Glancing up, he smiled at his sister, Tiffany. "You made it."

She rolled her eyes. "It would take an asteroid hitting the earth and causing a massive disaster to keep me away from my nephew."

She reached his side and he offered his son. "Well, you should feel special. No one has held him but me, Gaby, and medical staff so far."

Gaby sighed. "Mom is going to remind you of this for the rest of time."

He grinned at his mate. "She can be first the next time."

Tiffany took Mateo and cooed at him. She whispered, "I'm your Aunt Tiffy. We're going to have a lot of fun in the future. No matter what trouble you get into, just call me and we'll work it out."

As he watched his sister mumble baby words and nonsense at his son, he wrapped an arm around Gaby's shoulders. The two most important women in his life were here, as well as all of the family that had adopted them as his own.

True, he may have lost a brother in the last few years, but he'd gained enough family to fill a small restaurant. And despite their eccentricities, he loved them all.

However, as he stared down at his mate, he loved her most of all. "You are my heart, Gaby."

She leaned against him. "And you're part of my very soul."

As they merely sat there and watched everyone else take a turn with their son, Ryan knew his life was a good one. And no matter what it took, he'd do anything to keep and protect what was his.

The Dragon's Bidder

TAHOE DRAGON MATES #3

In exchange for favors to help his clan, PineRock's dragon leader Wes Dalton agrees to participate in a charity auction. After all, one evening dining or dancing with one lucky bidder shouldn't be too hard to endure. Then he notices the true mate he can never have in the audience—Ashley Swift. When she wins him for the night, the battle begins between what his dragon half wants and what his human half tries to deny.

Ashley Swift worked her way up the ranks of the American Department of Dragon Affairs and knows the ins and outs of dragon-shifters in her area. And while it's against the rules and she knows it, Ashley is drawn to PineRock's clan leader. They've danced around each other for years, but Ashley finally found a way to spend an evening with Wes—a charity auction. Nothing in the rules prevents her from bidding, and she wins. One night is all she needs to get him out of her system, or so she tries to tell herself.

As the pair dance around their undeniable attraction to one another, more than Ashley's job or Wes's position is at stake. They stumble upon something brewing in Reno and it's up to them to stop it. Only then can they think of a way to skirt the rules and be together.

NOTE: This is a quick, steamy standalone story about fated mates and sexy dragon-shifters near Lake Tahoe in the USA. You don't have to read all my other dragons books to enjoy this one!

The paperback version will be available by the end of July 2020.

The Conquest

KELDERAN RUNIC WARRIORS #1

Leader of a human colony planet, Taryn Demara has much more on her plate than maintaining peace or ensuring her people have enough to eat. Due to a virus that affects male embryos in the womb, there is a shortage of men. For decades, her people have enticed ships to their planet and tricked the men into staying. However, a ship hasn't been spotted in eight years. So when the blip finally shows on the radar, Taryn is determined to conquer the newcomers at any cost to ensure her people's survival.

Prince Kason tro de Vallen needs to find a suitable planet for his people to colonize. The Kelderans are running out of options despite the fact one is staring them in the face —Planet Jasvar. Because a group of Kelderan scientists disappeared there a decade ago never to return, his people dismiss the planet as cursed. But Kason doesn't believe in curses and takes on the mission to explore the planet to prove it. As his ship approaches Jasvar, a distress signal chimes in and Kason takes a group down to the planet's surface to explore. What he didn't expect was for a band of females to try and capture him.

As Taryn and Kason measure up and try to outsmart each other, they soon realize they've found their match. The only question is whether they ignore the spark between them and focus on their respective people's survival or can they find a path where they both succeed?

The paperback version of *The Conquest* is available now!

Author's Note

I hope you enjoyed Gaby and Ryan's story! By now you're probably chomping at the bit to read about Wes and Ashley. Well, good news! Their story is next. *The Dragon's Bidder* will be releasing July 16, 2020. (You have jury duty to blame for it not being out in June. Sigh.) I had originally planned only three stories in this series to see how people liked them, mostly because they're a little over half the length of my other books. However, so far this novella series seems popular! So I might be writing a few more stories. I don't know if it'll be about other people on PineRock, or about some of the dragons living on the other three clans near Lake Tahoe. We'll see what ideas come to mind for me! Regardless, thanks for following this new series of mine. Novellas are a nice break for me from writing longer, more complicated stories. :)

And now I have some people to thank for getting this out into the world:

- To Becky Johnson and her team at Hot Tree Editing. I've become a better writer because of Becky, and her team helps find extra typos and inconsistencies.
- To all my beta readers—Sabrina D., Donna H., Sandy H., and Iliana G., you do an amazing job at finding those lingering typos and minor inconsistencies.

And as always, a huge thank you to you, the reader, for either enjoying my dragons for the first time, or for following me from my longer books to this series. Writing is the best job in the world and it's your support that makes it so I can keep doing it.

Until next time, happy reading!

The Dragon's Dilemma (LHD #1)

The Dragon Guardian (LHD #2)

The Dragon's Heart (LHD #3)

The Dragon Warrior (LHD #4)

The Dragon Family (LHD #5)

The Dragon's Discovery (LHD #6)

The Dragon's Pursuit (LHD #7)

The Dragon Collective / Cat & Lachlan (LHD #8 / TBD)

Love in Scotland

Crazy Scottish Love (LiS #1)

Chaotic Scottish Wedding (LiS #2)

Stonefire Dragons

Sacrificed to the Dragon (SD #1)

Seducing the Dragon (SD #2)

Revealing the Dragons (SD #3)

Healed by the Dragon (SD #4)

Reawakening the Dragon (SD #5)

Loved by the Dragon (SD #6)

Surrendering to the Dragon (SD #7)

Cured by the Dragon (SD #8)

Aiding the Dragon (SD #9)

Finding the Dragon (SD #10)

Craved by the Dragon (SD #11)

Persuading the Dragon / Zain and Ivy (SD #12 / May 2020)

Stonefire Dragons Shorts

Meeting the Humans (SDS #1)

The Dragon Camp (SDS #2)

The Dragon Play (SDS #3)

Stonefire Dragons Universe

Winning Skyhunter (SDU #1)

Transforming Snowridge (SDU #2)

Tahoe Dragon Mates

The Dragon's Choice (TDM #1)

The Dragon's Need (TDM #2)

The Dragon's Bidder (TDM #3 / July 2020)

WRITING AS LIZZIE ENGLAND

Her Fantasy

Holt: The CEO

Callan: The Highlander

Adam: The Duke

Gabe: The Rock Star

About the Author

Jessie Donovan has sold over half a million books, has given away hundreds of thousands more to readers for free, and has even hit the *NY Times* and *USA Today* bestseller lists. She is best known for her dragon-shifter series, but also writes about elemental magic users, alien warriors, and even has a crazy romantic comedy series set in Scotland. When not reading a book, attempting to tame her yard, or traipsing around some foreign country on a shoestring, she can often be found interacting with her readers on Facebook. She lives near Seattle, where, yes, it rains a lot but it also makes everything green.

Visit her website at: www.JessieDonovan.com

Printed in Poland
by Amazon Fulfillment
Poland Sp. z o.o., Wrocław

58550754R00099